"Why have you come back?" Marcie asked.

"I want you," Ray said.

She blushed, hot and deep, then froze as he kissed her.

Her mouth was pressed tight shut. It didn't matter. He took his time, tasting her lips, nibbling and exploring the soft skin of her cheek and neck until he was close enough to inhale the fragrance of her hair, the perfume behind her ear unleashed by heat.

"Do I scare you that much?"

Her mouth was dry, her heart thudded against her ribcage. "It's not as simple as just wanting."

"Make love with me again, find out."

"No!" She pushed him away. He barely moved. But she'd broken the spell. "There's a difference between nostalgia and going into heat."

"This is about wanting what we had once, what we can have again, Marcie. Prove me wrong. Show me memory is better than any reality we might have."

A challenge, a taunt. If _____ how close she was to heeding _____ the dark that promised _____ she'd only dared dream _____

WHAT ARE *LOVESWEPT* ROMANCES?

They are stories of true romance and touching emotion. We believe those two very important ingredients are constants in our highly sensual and very believable stories in the *LOVESWEPT* line. Our goal is to give you, the reader, stories of consistently high quality that may sometimes make you laugh, sometimes make you cry, but are always fresh and creative and contain many delightful surprises within their pages.

Most romance fans read an enormous number of books. Those they truly love, they keep. Others may be traded with friends and soon forgotten. We hope that each *LOVESWEPT* romance will be a treasure—a "keeper." We will always try to publish

LOVE STORIES YOU'LL NEVER FORGET
BY AUTHORS YOU'LL ALWAYS REMEMBER

The Editors

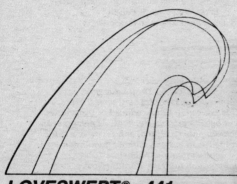

LOVESWEPT® • 441

Terry Lawrence
Unfinished Passion

 BANTAM BOOKS
NEW YORK • TORONTO • LONDON • SYDNEY • AUCKLAND

UNFINISHED PASSION
A Bantam Book / December 1990

LOVESWEPT® and the wave device are registered
trademarks of Bantam Books, a division of
Bantam Doubleday Dell Publishing Group, Inc.
Registered in U.S. Patent
and Trademark Office and elsewhere.

If you would be interested in receiving protective vinyl
covers for your Loveswept books, please write to this
address for information:

Loveswept
Bantam Books
P. O. Box 985
Hicksville, NY 11802

ISBN 0-553-44072-1

Published simultaneously in the United States and Canada

Bantam Books are published by Bantam Books, a division
of Bantam Doubleday Dell Publishing Group, Inc. Its trademark, consisting of the words "Bantam Books" and the
portrayal of a rooster, is Registered in U.S. Patent and
Trademark Office and in other countries. Marca Regis-
trada. Bantam Books, 666 Fifth Avenue, New York, New
York 10103.

PRINTED IN THE UNITED STATES OF AMERICA

OPM   0 9 8 7 6 5 4 3 2 1

One

"Marcella Courville." The court clerk set down the curling slip of paper with Marcie's name on it. Marcie stood, smoothed the skirt of her navy suit, and tucked her bag under her arm. She walked across the courtroom.

She always did have impeccable posture, Ray Crane thought. Breeding showed. In Marcie's world, breeding mattered.

With his feet in the aisle, Ray tilted the plastic chair back until its front legs were a couple of inches off the ground. Gently rocking it with his heel, he watched her step up into the jury box, turn left, and sidle down to the first seat. It took effort to remind himself he was there for jury duty, not to watch her fanny move—nor to watch her cross her legs. Considering she now sat behind a paneled wooden railing, that would be impossible to see. But not to imagine, Ray mused. She'd always had sexy legs.

In the ten years since he'd last seen her, she had filled out in a few more places—good places—

places a man would like to get his hands on. The word *breeding* occurred to him again. With a thud, Ray brought the chair legs down to the carpet.

He hadn't come back to town because of Marcie. He doubted she even remembered him. Running his thumb across the waist of his slacks, he knew she wasn't the only one who'd filled out a little. When she'd known him, he'd still been a lean and lanky boy. Sometimes he wondered if she'd ever really seen him as a man.

Sure she had, he told himself. He'd been a man she'd needed to use. He'd done the leaving, she'd done the letting go.

"Ray Crane," the clerk said, flattening the slip of paper under the palm of her hand as if it were a bug on a countertop.

Marcie Courville turned her head, her eyes wide. Ray doused a grin as he started down the aisle, knowing she watched him every step of the way. She did remember. Apparently those memories held all the pleasantness of finding a cockroach on a wedding cake.

He didn't have to look up to see that cameo face, shimmering blond hair, wide blue eyes flecked with gold. Some things never changed.

He let himself through the swinging gate dividing the court from the spectators. In two loping strides he was past a lawyers' table, in another four he was over the navy-and-rose carpet woven with the coat of arms of the state of Michigan and up the step to the jury box, where he sidestepped all the way down to the empty seat beside her.

Right away he was uncomfortable. He either had to pull up his knees, bump the wooden rail in front of him, or slant them to the left—or the right toward Marcie. He couldn't slouch, not the way he had before his name had been called, when half his attention had been on the selection procedure, the other half on the back of Marcie's neck.

He'd been engrossed by the tendrils of butter-blond hair floating across her nape. She had soft, sloping shoulders, a swanlike neck. Her hair was in an intricate French braid that ended in a small bun, like an exclamation point punctuated by a fat period. It made him think of the definitive "shush" he sensed coming his way when he swung his legs to the right, looped his fingers together in his lap, and said, "Hello, Marcella."

"Hello, Ray."

While he'd been sitting in the audience studying the back of her head, he'd wondered how he could have recognized her so quickly after ten years. Listening to the echo of her voice playing in his brain, he wondered how he ever could have forgotten her. He used to say her voice was whiskey smooth. She used to laugh.

She wasn't laughing now.

The clerk announced another name, Dozier.

"Are we choosing alphabetically today?" Judge Rosen asked testily. "Courville, Crane, Dozier. It'll be Edwards next."

The clerk smiled wanly and pulled another name from the drum with a satisfied snap. "Zylowski."

There were scattered chuckles among the spectators. Ray barely heard them. He would've taken bets Marcie didn't either. She faced forward, gaze apparently riveted on the state flag. Whatever she saw, it was giving her fits, and she'd be damned if she'd let it show. Typical.

Ray grunted and pulled his elbows in as the third juror took her seat. It gave him a chance to shift over, leaning across the armrest to speak a few quiet words. "I said hello."

"And I said hello in return." It would have had more effect if she'd said it to him and not the middle distance between them and the judge's bench.

"Is that all you're going to say?"

She licked her lips with a flick of her tongue, not wetting them enough to take the sheen off her pearl-pink lipstick, but just enough to make Ray think again about how cramped his legs were.

"This is jury selection, not a class reunion," she replied, her gaze flickering over his face, then back to the railing in front of them. He thought he sensed her immediate regret at sounding so harsh, but he might have imagined it. Either way, she was quickly behind the cool facade again.

"Ah well." He hitched up his belt and tried to get comfortable, but a six-foot-four man had few options, considering the space. "As I recall I never was in your class, Marcie."

He felt her tense. Score one, he thought. Grinning, Ray glanced at the judge, the clerk, the spectators, and back to her. "I think we can visit a bit. They're still calling names."

From the stiff cast to her shoulders, he supposed she had some choice names she'd like to call him.

He was more intrigued than insulted. How did she manage it? Marcie managed to be tactful and cool, thoughtful and polite, even when inviting a man out of her life. Ten years after the fact, he wasn't sure if he thanked her for that or held it against her. He suspected—no dammit, he knew—that beneath her smooth exterior there were a hundred tangled emotions, feelings she rarely showed.

Jury selection continued until a full panel of twelve was chosen. Ray stared at the woodwork in the refurbished century-old courthouse, the new vinyl window casings, the light fixtures with their big, round globes and green ironwork casings molded to look like leaves holding fat, white grapes. He tried to estimate the construction costs, what he would've bid on the job, but his mind wasn't up to the game. Emotions of his own interfered with what was usually an uncluttered business sense.

Emotions. Ray liked to think his were as blunt and easy to follow as a AAA road map. Marcie was unfinished business. Her memory had been dogging him too long. It was time to settle the bill.

He'd been twenty-four that summer, doing construction work for his uncle Ted. She'd been nineteen—young, pretty, a girl to fill any man's fantasies. Willful, serious minded, Marcie had been just rebellious enough to go after what she'd wanted—and she'd wanted him.

Exactly why a girl who had everything would want him seemed as mysterious and miraculous as their first kiss. He was flattered, gullible, and too eager to be used to realize it wasn't love at first sight. It wasn't even lust. Marcella Courville had decided she didn't want to be a virgin anymore. And Ray Crane had been glad to oblige.

A juror in the upper row knocked the back of

his chair, jolting him back to the present. "Sorry. Excuse me."

"No problem." Ray rearranged himself again, resting a foot on one knee, absently rubbing his ankle, inconspicuously tugging up his sock.

No doubt about it. The woman Marcie had become would have access to a better class of man. Of course, she'd had access to them then. But she'd picked him. And when the summer had ended, they'd gone their separate ways—or so he liked to think. He glanced over at that delicate profile, wondering if she'd told herself the same lies.

Ray studied the alabaster skin of the woman beside him. It took him a moment to realize that scars like the ones he was looking for didn't show.

"So how have you been?"

"Ray, could this perhaps wait until later?"

"Sure. Maybe we could have a drink."

That almost won him a look. She'd left him an opening and now she was paying for it. Judging from the clutch and release she was doing with the purse in her lap, she was having one hell of an argument with herself. She sensed him watching and set the purse beside her thigh. Crossing her legs, she used the motion to turn away from him. That was okay, it gave him more room to stretch his legs her way.

"Think this'll take long?" he asked conversationally.

"No, I—" she began.

"Takes forever," an older man grumbled two seats away. "Third jury I've been called on."

Marcella flushed, forcing her fingers to relax. Ray hadn't even been talking to her.

Why hadn't she heard he was back in town?

The layer of sun-bleached blond that had topped his hair like a crown was gone. It was now a burnished brown, highlighted with a few startling strands of gray at his temples. It galled her that she missed the gold. At twenty-four he'd looked like an ad for suntan lotion, beer, a man's cologne, anything male, sexual, muscled, or slick.

She'd wanted him so badly, she'd ached. She'd also loved him so much. . . .

The judge sent someone into his chambers to fetch something. Ray chatted with the woman beside him. This close Marcie could almost smell the cologne, count the razor-trimmed hairs on the back of his neck just above his white collar. His skin was tanned a deep brown. The crinkles around his eyes had become fans etched into his temples. He had a wide mouth; the dimples replaced by permanent lines that cut into his cheeks, familiar signposts on a rugged face. She'd kissed every one of them, with mouth closed, with mouth open.

She'd run then, frightened by the intensity of her feelings. And if they had it to do over again? A small voice in her head challenged her, The truth and nothing but the truth, Marcie. She smiled ruefully.

He turned, caught her looking, and grinned. She faced front.

"Thank you for your patience, ladies and gentlemen. I'd like to welcome you to circuit court. I'm Judge Edward Rosen. We're here to try a felony case."

The jurors nodded.

"I would like to begin by asking if any of you have any conflicts that would prevent you from sitting on a jury during the month of March. You will be asked to sit on only one panel, for a case expected to last approximately two weeks."

Most shook their heads.

"No conflicts?"

Marcie had a conflict all right, she just wasn't sure how to phrase it. She wasn't afraid of being near Ray. Her out-of-control passion was a memory . . . yet it clung. She'd shown him so much of herself, lows and highs she hadn't known she was capable of.

She'd thrown herself at him, she thought with a flush, gripping the smooth wooden armrest. Did he remember? Had he laughed at her eagerness then? He was grinning as if he knew a secret. Oh yes. Marcie Courville, who prided herself on her poise, had made a fool of herself over Ray Crane. She'd vowed it would never happen again.

The painful part was that she'd been so sure he'd shared her love, until he'd left without so much as a backward glance.

"Are any of you planning vacations?" the judge asked.

One woman raised her hand. After a lengthy personal explanation, plus some grumbling from the judge concerning the necessity for all to serve when called, he allowed her to step down. Another name was chosen. A middle-aged woman took her seat.

"Any other scheduling conflicts?"

"Your Honor, I run a business," Marcella said, half rising out of her seat.

"Yes, Miss Courville?"

She'd changed back to her maiden name. Ray'd heard that earlier, he noted it now. She'd been married eight years ago, divorced six. He'd carried the two newspaper clippings in his wallet until the wallet fell apart. If she'd had children, nobody'd told him.

The judge continued his questioning. "Do you have any employees, Miss Courville?"

"Yes, I have a partner."

"And what does he or she do?"

"She deals with customers, estimates job expenses, orders supplies."

"Sounds like she can run the business in your absence. What is the nature of the work?"

"Custom woodwork, window trim. We specialize in restoration of historical homes, doors, mantelpieces, some tables."

"Thanks for the ad," the judge murmured wryly.

The spectators chuckled.

"As far as I'm aware, March is a slow month for home construction. I won't excuse you for that. Anyone else?"

Marcie sat back down, the corners of her mouth tight. She did that when she didn't get her way.

Ray studied his shoes and the unexpected stab of memory. So much was coming back to him. Except for the woman herself.

"The case we'll have before us concerns embezzlement," the judge continued. "Has anyone on this jury ever been accused of embezzlement?"

A young woman at the other end raised her hand.

"Want to tell me about it, Miss Swanson?"

The woman addressed her words to the design in the carpet. "When I was sixteen, I—I was accused of taking money out of the till at the party store where I worked."

"Was it true?"

"Yes, sir," she answered, eyes downcast.

"Were the police involved?"

"No, sir! I paid it all back, and it never happened again."

"Do you think that would influence your judgment in this case?"

"Depends on the facts of the case, sir."

"Sounds fair enough to me. Anyone else?"

The panel shook their heads no.

"What about employers? Miss Courville, you run a business. Have you, or anyone else on the panel, ever had an employee, relative, or acquaintance charged with embezzlement?"

Ray raised his hand. "I've had employees caught stealing. More than once."

"Same employee?"

"They don't do it twice and work for me."

"Mmm," the judge said, glancing at the attorneys' tables. "Care to elaborate?"

"I own a construction company. Some people get the idea leftover materials are theirs to cart home. Same with power tools."

"Ever bring any of them to trial?"

"We settled it between ourselves."

The growl in Ray's voice brought smiles to a number of faces. The judge hid his behind his hand and gave Ray's juror questionnaire a quick going over. "You don't have to go into the details here, Mr. Crane."

"Thank you."

"Anyone else? What about employment history? Have any of you ever been fired without what you felt was just cause?"

No answers.

"Not even you, young lady?" The judge patted

down the hairs combed across his bald spot while waiting for the young ex-thief's reply.

"They let me stay."

"Good. No others? We must have a very honest and competent jury here. All right, I'm going to go over the rules of testimony, then turn you over to the attorneys. Do any of you know either of the attorneys present, or have you conducted business with the firms they represent?"

A number of jurors raised their hands. Marcie raised hers. "I know the prosecuting attorney, Your Honor, and the owner of the company involved. They're members of the country club."

"As am I." The judge smiled. "Well, this is a small town, so the chances of any of you knowing someone involved are fairly good. The question is, can you maintain your objectivity? Miss Courville, have you discussed the case with either of the people you know?"

"No, sir."

"All right. Mr. Spannick is the prosecuting attorney. Mr. Hazelton is the defense attorney. If any of you see either of these men in the hall, you are not to speak to them regarding this case. If any of the witnesses approach you, you don't speak to them, not to point out the washrooms, not to give them the time of day. Any approach by a witness to a juror is considered jury tampering and must be reported to me immediately. Not my secretary, not the court clerk, but to me. Do you understand? Good."

"Your Honor?"

"Yes, Miss Courville?" He sighed.

"What about jurors talking to jurors?"

Ray shifted in his seat. He hadn't seen that one coming.

"If jurors couldn't talk to each other, Miss Courville, they'd never reach a verdict. Although I have had some juries like that."

The spectators laughed, as did all of the jury except for two.

"Ladies and gentlemen, despite what you've seen on TV, this will not be a sequestered case. Jurors can go about their business when court is not in session, and can discuss anything outside the courtroom except the case itself. You are enjoined, that means forbidden, to read anything about the case in newspapers or view it on television. Understood?"

Marcie nodded, readjusting the purse on her lap. The corners of her mouth were tighter than ever.

"Good try," Ray whispered, and grinned. "You almost got off."

She glared at him. "This is serious."

"What we had wasn't?"

Her stare cooled abruptly, the look in her eyes either pain or caution.

She was caught. If she looked away now, he'd know how eager she was to run.

The judge's voice broke the spell. "Do any of you feel in any way prejudiced against someone merely for being charged with a crime? No? Then before I turn you over to the attorneys, does anyone else have any reason to feel he or she could not serve on this jury?"

Marcie twisted her fingers, lifted her chin, and continued to glare at Ray.

"Last chance," he whispered, the crease on the right side of his mouth deepening. That was the only indication that he was joking. The rest of his expression was deadly serious.

He wasn't her last chance, Marcie thought furiously, but he had been her first. She'd asked him to go, then resented that he had. She wasn't proud of the way she'd done it, or of the reasons she'd used. But she wasn't that girl anymore. She could sit in judgment on this case, thigh to thigh with Ray Crane if need be. The fact that he was enjoying watching her squirm only hardened her resolve.

"All right then," the judge pronounced. "Will the attorneys step forward?"

First one, then the other attorney asked questions of the panel. Mr. Hazelton began with, "How many married men are there here?"

Marcie didn't see the relevance, but she immediately sensed Ray's tension. Slowly, his hand rose. She felt as if her spinal column were a block of ice, capable of cracking with any motion.

"And what does your wife do?" the attorney asked.

"Do? Oh, I'm not married now. Divorced." Ray lowered his hand.

"That was going to be my next question. Are there any divorced people on the panel? Mr. Crane, was yours recent?"

"Twelve years ago."

"High school sweethearts, eh?" The young man's unctuous tone did nothing for Ray, who stared at Hazelton stonily until he pulled a maroon handkerchief from his vest pocket and wiped his sweaty palms. "Other divorces?" Of twelve jurors, seven raised their hands, Marcie included.

"The reason I ask is that I want you to remember during the course of this trial what it's like to be married. Few of us are ever judged by a jury. However, most of us do have that little lady to answer to when we get home at night." He chuckled. A couple of jurors joined him.

"Or little man as the case might be," he added lamely. "Okay then!" He practically clapped his hands together. "Just want you to keep that in mind."

After a few more questions, the judge asked if there were any removals for cause.

The young ex-thief was removed. Another name was called, and the newly picked juror went through the same series of questions from the judge.

"Preemptory challenges, gentlemen?"

"None, Your Honor."

"Mr. Hazelton?"

"None, Your Honor."

There was a surprised pause. "Well, then we continue as chosen. The rest of you can turn in your juror badges with the clerk—"

Ray enclosed Marcie's white hand in his heavy, callused one on the armrest. He'd been wanting to do that ever since she'd stopped wringing her fingers and had gotten up the courage to put her hand there. He gave it a squeeze. "Looks like we'll be seeing each other again."

Marcie rose half out of her seat. "Excuse me, Your Honor."

"Yes, Miss Courville?"

The jurors not chosen paused in their exodus for the door.

"I think there may be a reason why I can't be a juror. Mr. Crane and I knew each other a long time ago."

"That's not unusual in a town this size."

"Yes, well . . ."

Judge Rosen smiled, patted the hair combed

across his bald spot once more, and looked Marcella Courville up and down, from the leather bag clutched to her side to the trim navy suit. Pursing his lips in judicial contemplation, he gave Ray Crane a glance. For all his easy jocularity on the bench, he was a sharp and perceptive man. "I don't really want to get into this in court, Miss Courville, and I doubt you do. May I simply ask whether or not you would feel able to judge the facts of the case, as they are presented, without undue, ah, interference or, shall we say, broken concentration?"

Marcie was blushing fiercely. Everyone in the courtroom was eyeing her now. She straightened her shoulders, mustering all her dignity. "I'm sure I can."

"Then there's no problem, is there?" He nodded formally to the court at large, "Ladies and gentlemen, we have a jury."

Two

Marcie clutched her bag to her chest as she drove out of the parking lot. She was embarrassed. She'd practically revealed her love life to a room full of strangers.

She prided herself on her reserve. Friends confided in her precisely because she was so self-contained. But after one hour in Ray Crane's presence, that smooth surface trembled as if with the aftershocks of an earthquake. Maybe no one had any idea what she'd been referring to. She knew Ray had. She should have never let him know how much seeing him affected her.

Then again, if she counted the things she should have never done with Ray Crane, it would be a long list.

Things had changed, she told herself. She was a woman now, not a girl who dreamed and planned a life around a man who could leave and never look back. In ten years he hadn't tried to reach her once. She lived in the same town, the same house. . . .

He had tried to strike up a conversation, her conscience pointed out. She hadn't been very helpful.

She snapped off the car radio with a flick of her wrist and yanked up the parking brake, halting beside the carriage house that served as office and work space for Designs on the Past. Formerly a three-car garage, it had been a stable before that, back when her grandparents' estate had been home to the wealthiest family in Derby.

Marcie dragged open one side of the two-part garage door. The whine of an electric saw cut through the air. "Forty-five degrees," she called out, "can you believe it? It's practically summer. Let's get some fresh air in here!"

"You're back." Setting down the saw, her partner, Sandy, lifted her safety glasses onto her head like a headband, emphasizing the streak of white in her jet-black hair.

They couldn't have made a more unlikely pair, Marcie thought. She'd always had to-die-for blond hair and skin that tanned in the shortest of Michigan summers. Sandy was ebony and cream. It was Sandy who'd stuck that label on her: self-contained.

"Well?" her partner asked.

Marcie fidgeted with her French braid; her hair was coiled less tightly than she was. "I got picked."

"Pooh. Will it be an interesting case?"

While Marcie contemplated how a woman as sultry and sophisticated as Alexandra Mears Ingham could use a word like *pooh*, she set her purse down, hung up her suit jacket, and slipped on an apple-green smock. "Embezzlement."

"Mmm. Not as good as murder, but could be interesting."

"These are real people we're talking about."

"Which will make it even juicier than fiction. Were they there? Did the defendant's family arrive en masse, his bereft wife with babe in arms to sway your sympathy?"

"Family?" Marcie remembered her reaction when Ray had mistakenly answered the question about marriage. "I didn't notice."

Sandy gaped openly. "How could you not?"

Having owned this business for five years, Marcie knew how to fidget and make it look like work. She sorted through a pile of bills. How could she admit she'd spent most of the afternoon with her attention fixed on the man beside her? She grabbed an invoice instead. "How's the Walton job going?"

They were refinishing a long-abandoned farmhouse for a family named Walton. It was usually the source of at least one wisecrack from Sandy. Unfortunately, Marcie's timing was off; she'd changed the subject too fast. Sandy merely stood there studying her.

"I thought we could use some fresh air," Marcie explained unnecessarily, glancing out the door. The overhead furnace might be pumping out more heat than usual, but the business was doing fine, and they could afford the small luxury. Besides, Marcie needed the change of subject almost as much as the change of seasons. Spring meant fresh starts. She ran a hand up and down one arm, fighting off goose bumps.

She clutched at another invoice. If there was one thing she was good at, it was diving head first into work—and staying there, as Sandy so often complained.

"The Walton's contractor was on the phone this morning before I left for court, asking about those trim pieces. Like I did a minute ago? Hint, hint?"

"Think that's him coming down the drive?" Sandy asked.

"Drat." Marcella was in no mood to argue with short-tempered contractors.

She glanced through the east window and saw the car parked beside the gate. A bronze Mercedes. Then she heard a step on the gravel. He was almost at the door. That fast, Marcie's heart was in her throat. She'd heard those steps quietly crossing gravel on too many secret nights not to recognize them.

Ray Crane filled up the doorway. "Ladies."

"Mr. Crane," Marcie said, her voice steady, her hands folded. She even had her head tipped a little to one side in polite but not overeager interest. In her mind she could see her mother doing exactly the same thing when ambushed by a brush salesman the maid hadn't intercepted first. At certain uncomfortable moments manners were indispensible—and also easy to hide behind. Marcie looked him in the eye. Her first order of business was to dispel any notion he might have that she was still that star-struck girl.

"I was wondering if I could come in?" he asked, his voice rumbling softly into the room.

"Certainly."

He stepped across the threshold, his suit coat draped over one arm, his tie loosened at the knot and left to hang. "Marcie."

They simply looked at each other.

"Excuse me," Sandy said brightly, cutting

through the tension. Hefting a half dozen slats of trim, she headed out the door.

"Need some help carrying those?" Ray offered.

"Nope, just loading them in my truck. Excuse me, please."

"Let me." Ray stepped outside with her.

Marcie stopped mentally condemning Sandy for running out on her and silently thanked her for the brief reprieve. Somehow Sandy had sensed that Ray would no sooner stand by and let a woman carry something heavy than he'd . . . but how would she know what Ray did nowadays? Sandy's maneuver merely tacked a few extra minutes onto ten years.

Marcie listened to the truck start up, then rattle down the drive.

"She says to tell you she'll be at Walton Mountain," Ray said as he sauntered back in the half-opened door. "Is that a joke?"

Marcie found a proper smile to match his. "Afraid not," she replied. "That's what the owners call it."

"So." He wasn't going to fill up the space, the time, or the distance of years with chatter. Maybe he remembered that Marcie was no likelier to endure a silence than he was to let a woman lift slats of wood.

"I was surprised to see you today."

"Needless to say." He grinned. The lines in his face deepened.

Marcie's skin flushed. All right, so she'd been caught dreadfully off balance, that didn't mean he had to know how shaken up she remained. She'd done a lot of growing up, she could handle this now. "I didn't even know you were in town."

"Been here a while."

That could mean weeks or months. The fact that she hadn't known was strangely upsetting.

"Ever been on a jury before?" he asked.

Only when I judged you, she thought. But she'd kicked herself long enough for that mistake.

Her fingers plucked at the pile of receipts on the rolltop desk she'd spent so many hours refinishing. "I was called for a drunk driving case a few years ago. He pleaded guilty before it came to trial."

Fidgeting was pointless. He'd always seen right through her. But then, he'd never minded looking.

He watched her now, a half smile on his face, a knowing curious look in his eyes.

"This one might be more interesting." His voice was the same, maybe a little deeper. He was a tall, strapping man. The lankiness was gone, strength and breadth gained in return.

His eyes were still hazel, but warier, more cautious. She looked away, not wanting to risk seeing in them things she might have missed, pain she might have caused—or the complete lack of either.

"Are you staying in Derby long?" she asked.

"Hotel guests seldom get picked for jury duty."

"Of course, you're right."

"I put my name on a lease six months ago. Got my driver's license changed. That's where they get their names now. Then an emergency project came up in Akron. I've barely had time to get my furniture shipped. Lucky I got here when I did, or I would've missed my notice to appear. They'd have had the sheriff after me."

"Hardly," she joined in his chuckle. Judging from the Mercedes parked at the gate, the police weren't likely to stop this respectable, if raffish-looking, businessman for anything other than a speeding ticket.

"Do you still drive too fast?"

He nodded slowly, as if he were giving her words far too much importance. "To get from one project to another. Too bad tickets aren't tax write-offs. They're definitely a business expense for me. You're looking good, Marcie," he said with quiet conviction.

She was sure she looked hassled, harried, and as if she dreaded having a conversation with him, but she nodded her thanks. "You're looking fine yourself. It was kind of you to stop by." She was trying to convey indifference, or polite affection, but her stilted delivery was a dead giveaway.

He cleared his throat, tugging at his tie. "I wondered whether you still lived here. Mind if I look around?"

It was a real workshop, not a showplace filled with pieces shipped in for retail sale. Antique doors stripped from old houses leaned against the walls. The equipment was top-notch and clearly put to use. Plastic safety glasses hung over one workbench, while brush handles stuck out of jars of turpentine and chemical strippers. An efficient ventilation system kept the fumes from being overpowering, but even without it Ray wouldn't have minded. He'd lived around the smells of new construction all his life, and he loved working with wood.

Run your hand down that. The words came back to him, the sight of Marcie at nineteen, her long-fingered, pale hand skimming the flank of an oak door that had been hand sanded to a whispery smoothness, the grain dry and feathery to the touch. Ray had spread on a coat of stain.

The wood had drank it in, coming to golden life, rich, burnished, alive. Their hands had touched.

Ray cleared his throat, put his hands on his waist as he made a tour of the facility. "I see you love wood too."

Wood was easy, Marcie thought. If you treated it right, it showed. "We do custom woodworking, stripping, restoration, and all the beveled-glass doors we can rescue. That's a turn-of-the-century fireplace mantel there."

He tried to hide a smile by glancing up at the multipaned skylight.

"May I ask why that's funny?" She didn't like the defensiveness in her voice, or the set of her shoulders. With a deep breath, she eased both.

"I can see for myself, Marcie. But like the judge said, thanks for the commercial." He winked at her, pleased to see the flustered way she brushed back a hair.

"Do I brag that much?"

He shrugged. "You didn't hand out business cards to the jury. That's something, I guess."

He got her to laugh. It was a start. Toward what, he didn't know.

The talking to he'd given himself on the drive over should have been enough. He was there to catch up on old times. Speeding through the streets of Derby, trying to unobtrusively follow her car from the courthouse parking lot hadn't been necessary. Driving ten miles over the speed limit wouldn't make up the distance of ten years. Passing the time wouldn't answer the question that once again echoed in his heart: *Had she ever loved him?*

"I thought we could talk a bit," he said.

"That's what we're doing," she replied pleasantly as she indicated the room with a wave of one small-boned wrist.

Through the tangy odor of sawdust, he could have sworn he smelled her perfume. Heated skin released a delicate aroma, the smell of excitement. Maybe it was his imagination, cool air mixing with the heavy dry air that descended from the heater overhead.

Maybe he wasn't over her at all, he thought.

"It's not as if old friends don't have some catching up to do," he repeated.

"No, it's not as if . . ."

He couldn't help noticing the way her voice trailed off as he hitched up a pant leg and put a foot on top of a sawhorse, leaning his elbow on his raised knee. The discarded suit coat draped from his hand, swayed between his legs. The suit was expensive. She probably remembered him quite differently, bare chested, wearing jeans—or wearing nothing.

She puttered with the porcelain doorknob on a newly stained door. He could almost feel the coolness when her hand closed over it. The lock's metal tongue had been worn smooth by the years. She pricked her finger against it.

Ray's stomach tightened. He glanced down, noticing the dust on his raised shoe. Had she seen that in the courtroom? He should've grabbed a rag and shined them on the way into the building. He fought the urge to do it now. He wasn't there to impress her. If he'd been a lawyer he could just ask the question. One simple question. But he hesitated, cast around for something else. "I'm surprised you remember that, about my driving."

She laughed and shook her head. "I remember that old truck you had."

"It's a Mercedes now."

"So I noticed," she replied evenly. "You must be doing very well."

He'd worked damned hard. It irked him to think he needed to prove it. He took a step back, peering into the rafters, not sure he liked what he saw. "You run this place yourself?"

"Alexandra's my partner."

"That's it?"

"I wanted a small company. More control that way." She was a woman in control, as long as she made that clear. "As it is, I couldn't employ any more. You can't make a fortune refinishing old woodwork."

"Nonsense. You could do anything you wanted, I always knew that. You had goals. I liked that about you," he added.

They let the word *like* hang in the air, let it twist and turn with the motes of dust.

Marcie broke the silence. "And your company?"

"Crane Corporation. We construct shopping centers, office buildings, and you *can* make a fortune at it. We're doing the Rocky Creek Mall, south of town."

"You're doing that?" She was clearly impressed.

Ray let it sink in, wondering if it would make a difference. "Wilkerson Associates got the bid, subcontracted the major portion to us."

"That's quite a project."

"Not the biggest we've ever done, but good enough." Okay, it felt good. The construction worker returning as a self-made man, walking back into her life.

"Won't it be hard to keep up while serving on a jury?"

"Still trying to get one of us off this jury?" She gave him a flashing, self-conscious smile. "Don't worry, my secretary already tried it." That had been before he'd had any idea who'd be on the jury with him. "With frost laws in effect through the beginning of April, we can't start excavations. The judge wouldn't let me off."

"You always planned on owning a big company," she said. "You were going to night school."

And she was making polite conversation. That might be all he'd get from her this time around. He was surprised to find himself already planning the next time. "So I was," he murmured. "Going to school, working . . ." And making time he didn't have to love her.

"You must be very proud."

"Does that mean I'm on your level now?" he asked quietly.

"Ray."

"I didn't suppose it would."

"That's not what I meant."

"I don't need to be told I'm suitable now that I have money, darlin'."

Her eyes were filled with icy fire. "You didn't need to come here to insult me after all this time."

He didn't answer, only watched as she wrapped the smock tightly around her, anchoring it with recrossed arms. Maybe, just maybe he'd found a way to penetrate that impeccable veneer.

"If this is my punishment, save it," she said, delicately pointed chin in the air. "I refuse to feel guilty over something I did as a girl ten years ago."

"Guilty?" His brows shot up in surprise. "Hell,

why should you feel guilty, Marcie? You were being true to your own values."

"Which I suppose you thought were shallow."

"Nineteen-year-olds aren't known for their depth."

He walked toward her, stopping only when he was so close she wanted to back away but didn't dare. "Then why are you back?"

"If not to punish you?" The notion made him smile. She was that same mix of determination and vulnerability. He'd never quite figured her out. Maybe that had been his downfall. He'd had one hell of a blind spot where Marcie Courville was concerned. Had he really been fooled into thinking she loved him? She'd used him, dumped him. So why these glimpses of hurt? Was she that good an actress or was he still that great a fool?

About the only thing he'd figured out so far was that standing close to her made his mouth dry.

He watched her swallow, the movement fluttering the pale column of her neck. Was she feeling it too? The tension of people who've known each other inside and out. Known feelings, fears, flesh. Known too much to play this cordial game. He saw what he needed to do.

"I came back because I wanted to say hello." He watched her eyes widen as he bent forward, his lips brushing hers. "Hello, Marcie."

Three

It should have been a kiss, nothing more. No doubt that was all he intended. There was no reason why Marcie's heartbeat should echo in her chest like hollow wood. A rush of blood whined in her ear like a saw cutting through something, her heart was spinning like the blade. When she opened her eyes he was already turning away, walking out of her life again. "Ray."

He stopped at the fireplace mantel. On tiptoe she'd had trouble stripping that upper corner; he merely lifted his hand and ran it over the light oak. "You're doing a nice job with this."

Was he actually retreating to normal conversation? Marcie closed her eyes and tried to shake his kiss, his smell, out of her memory, as a well of regret opened around her heart. It was so impossible to go back—and it would be so humiliating if he realized how much she longed to. She pulled herself together.

"A house was almost torn down with that in it," she said, mustering all her dignity. "Sandy and I got in touch with the owner at the last minute and took out everything of historical value." He was watching her in the mantel mirror. She thought she was doing fairly well, considering. "It's marvelous. Some people would design an entire house around that."

"You do this kind of thing a lot, then?"

"I like rescuing old pieces."

"Making things the way they were, is that it, Marcie?"

She stopped watching his hand move, her eyes drawn to his. It wasn't hard to remember how that hand had lingered over her body. Studious, admiring, fascinated, loving. Had it meant anything to him? "Some things can't be restored," she said, her voice so low it barely carried across the room.

"Good wood is always worth saving. Of course, with the antiques your parents had, you never had to scrape very deep to find quality, did you?"

She bristled. Why oh why was he so good at pushing the right buttons? He sauntered back into her life as easily as he'd left it, kissed her with just the right blend of tenderness, curiosity, and familiarity to set her heart skittering for cover, then he tossed her a grenade.

"So everything was easy for me, is that what you're saying?"

"I suppose so." Frank, blunt, daring her to let go, to lash out.

She wouldn't fall for it. "I'll admit my upbringing wasn't exactly difficult, but that doesn't mean everything was handed to me on a platter. After you left—"

"After I *what*?" His voice was low, his eyes hard.

She caught herself before emotion could clog her voice. Yes, she'd sent him away, but he hadn't fought it. Unmoved, uncaring, he'd gone. "It's been a long time," she stated carefully. "Things change."

"So tell me."

She shrugged, unwilling to let the conversation be anything more than an exchange of information. After all, she couldn't blurt out how much his stoniness had hurt. "Loved ones die in every family, money gets tight. That's life. I struggled to build my business, Ray. This wasn't handed to me."

He considered quietly. "Okay, I'll give you that."

"I don't need you to give me anything. I'm on my own. I've got my mother's care to think of, the house to deal with, a business to run. My life is very full."

"And you're full of it too."

She would've lashed out at him if it weren't for the sudden teasing in his eyes. She was being pompous and unnecessarily self-important. He always could get under her skin.

"There's only one thing you're missing, that I can see."

What she was missing didn't show, but she knew that wouldn't stop him from assuming. "My private life—"

"—is full, too, I'm sure." He leaned back and crossed his arms. "So why do you look like a woman who isn't getting any?"

"You're being purposely crude."

"Isn't that what attracted you to me in the first place?"

"No."

"There was more? I'm flattered."

"I meant, no, I don't want to get into this. Let's not dredge up the past."

"Like some kind of sewage?"

"No!" She put her palms against her cheeks, another gesture, another stab of memory for Ray.

"I always could get a rise out of you," he added softly, dangerously. He crossed one long leg over the other and continued to study her. They both knew how good it had been. "As I recall, I could prick that self-control of yours like a balloon."

"That's not the way I remember it."

"You want to talk about something else?"

"Please."

"All right. Why don't we just talk about how good we were in bed?"

She glared at him and bit off her words. "If you don't stop that, I'm going to ask you to leave."

"Ask."

"Leave."

"That sounds more like an order."

"I decided to skip the niceties."

"Now, Marcie, that's not like you." He grinned and winked. "Think I'll stay a bit longer. Who knows, I may even invite myself up to the house."

Her blood ran cold, pooling somewhere low inside her. "Why, Ray?"

It was an open question. Why was he back? Why did he insist on irritating her, taunting her? Kissing her?

He could have answered that one a dozen ways. But the truth was, he didn't know why he'd done it. Maybe it was the vulnerability he'd glimpsed, the fact that she wasn't immune to him. He might make her angry or cautious, but at least he could make her feel. Long past the dewy-eyed stage of seeing romance when it wasn't there, he was determined to make her show him.

He ran his hand over a cherry door. "Did I ever tell you that caring for wood is a lot like making love? Both require touch, moisture, protection, and tender loving care."

"No," she lied.

"Too bad. I thought it was one of my better lines." This time there was an unmistakable spark in her eye. He wanted sparks.

"Does it work?" she asked.

"Has more than once."

Her mouth thinned, turning down at the corners. That one had hit home. It shouldn't have. His love life was no business of hers. She marched over to a walnut and brass hall tree and plucked off her suit coat. "If you want to see the house, come on."

He didn't move from his spot by the mantel. After a moment he cleared his throat. "Your house?"

"Mine, my parents'." She waved a hand in the direction of Courville House.

It was barely a polite invitation. Ray knew how those went. One demurral from him, and she'd show him the door. "I don't know if they'd be keen on receiving me."

A strange sensation curled through Marcie as she realized that he didn't know about her parents. "Father died a few years ago, Mother's been moved to a nursing home. Just before Christmas."

"That must have been hard."

"She didn't really notice."

"I'm sorry, Marcie."

He was about to touch her again. Sympathy she couldn't deal with. She had to take action, crying in his arms was out of the question. It had been so hard, and she'd done it all alone. Suddenly it seemed more a sad fact of life than an accomplishment.

She hung up her smock and tested her vocal cords with a short cough. "We're turning the house into condominium apartments, six of them. I'm living in one now, the others will be sold. It's the only way we could retain the house in more or less its original condition. No one wanted it as a whole."

"You tried to sell it?"

She didn't answer directly. "I'll show you how far the renovations have come."

She was touching the back of her braid, head bowed, eyes unfocused as she tucked the loosened strands into place. It was such a womanly, unselfconscious thing to do. It was the intimate, unexpected things that had the most power to start up aches Ray hadn't felt in too long.

They walked down the path. Ray never had liked Courville House. Maybe it had something to do with always approaching it from the back, the working-class boy romancing the golden girl. A weeping willow rained icy droplets on their heads. Ray turned his collar up. As they rounded the corner he looked up and saw the damage.

The ground in front of the house was torn up everywhere. Deep gouges from construction equipment trailed across what had once been an impressive lawn stretching down the hill, overlooking all of Derby and beyond.

Ray pulled off his tie, scrunching it in his fist as an unwarranted feeling of victory surged through him. He'd prospered, and this is what

Courville House had come to. It was an unworthy reaction, but no less real.

The paint was chipped and bubbled, the intricate brick walkway was torn up in chunks, replaced by flagstones—serviceable, presentable, less expensive to install and maintain. The west garden was gone, paved over and covered by a carport big enough to house ten cars. Of course no one in town had been able to buy it whole, who could afford it? "Condos then."

"Yes."

They passed by each unit, following the long porch column by column, until they stood directly in front of the main entrance. Ray had never walked in that door. Never.

"I know it looks bad right now," Marcie said with false heartiness, "but once the landscaping is finished, and of course the painting—"

"Marcie, it's late."

"Pardon me?" She turned swiftly, startled by the gentleness in his voice.

"Maybe some other time."

It was plain she didn't catch his meaning. She'd been wrapped up in telling him the woes of construction. And he'd been cheering on every disrupted stone, every chipped pillar. Why? Was he there to break through walls? Dislocate and change everything until it was brought down to his level? The searing rush of ugly emotions disturbed him.

He wasn't there for revenge. He had to believe that. She was a woman now, not a carefree, careless girl. From the moment he'd seen her he'd wanted to touch her. Hell, he'd given in and kissed her. He wanted more. But would winning her in bed be enough? He knew it wouldn't. What was worse, he knew he'd settle for it.

Ray stepped off the bottom step. He never walked into anything without estimating the cost. Ever since Marcie, that included emotional costs. "I'm going to have to take a rain check on the tour."

Marcie folded her hands in front of her again, polite, self-contained, back in control. "Perhaps some other time, then."

"I'll walk myself back." That was his only good-bye. The last time she'd done the pursuing, until she'd lost interest. Now it was up to him to make the next move. But he'd have to think it through, plan his way. He was laying claim to everything the lady had to give. This time, he wouldn't take less.

"Why'd he kiss you?"

Two weeks after Ray had opted out of the house tour, Marcie considered Sandy's sensible question. Pride had to be the most damnable emotion! "I've been thinking the same thing."

"So why didn't you come right out and ask him?"

"Confrontation is your department, I'm afraid."

"You don't do so badly. I've seen you go after overdue accounts. You can charm the money right off the trees."

"Where Ray Crane thinks it grows for people like me."

"What does that mean?"

"I think he believes I let him go because of the difference in our classes."

"Why would he think that?"

"Because I let him." She laughed, a short, rueful laugh. "It was easier than the truth."

"You were crazy about him."

"Am I that transparent to everyone?"

Sandy put a hand on her shoulder. "Only your nearest and dearest. I think you scare everyone else away. It's that air of complete self-sufficiency. The I'll-Handle-It Woman."

"So I'm a fraud."

"No, there's just more to you than you let on to the world. You don't share yourself with just anybody. If Ray Crane knows that, he must have been pretty clued-in."

"Only because I threw myself at him." Marcie contemplated the raised grain on an old secretary. "I don't even know if he loved me. He never wrote or called . . ."

"Oh no!" Sandy gasped, standing at the saber saw.

Marcie froze, then broke into a run. "What's wrong?"

"Don't tell me this is one of those star-crossed lover things, where your mother or an evil housekeeper intercepted his letters! The workmen will find a cache of them behind a secret panel in the library. You two will be reconciled."

Marcie laughed. "Our library has no secret panels."

"Your family needs more sense of adventure. Why, if I owned that house, there'd be tunnels and false chiffoniers. You should put them in, it's not too late."

"And dungeons."

"For people who ignore RSVPs. Speaking of which, are you coming to my party?"

Marcie sighed. "Not if you're setting me up again."

"Scouts honor. Looks like Ray has your full attention for the time being."

Another sigh. "If only there'd been letters to intercept."

"Maybe he did care, and you hurt him so badly he never wrote. Did you break his fingers?"

Marcie didn't dignify that with an answer. "Maybe it was just friendliness. It wasn't exactly Rhett carrying Scarlett up the staircase."

"My kind of metaphor. Why do I get the idea that you have no intention of confronting Mr. Tall, Wide-Shouldered, and Handsome?"

"Because I don't. I'll let it slide this time."

How could she explain it wasn't the kiss, it was all the unsettled past behind it?

Her friends had teased her about being a virgin at the advanced age of nineteen. So she'd set a goal: to learn about love—the man-and-woman kind. Despite her carefully constructed plan, Marcella Lucy Courville didn't picture herself as calculating. She was simply being mature and levelheaded, as always.

Then she'd seen Ray nailing down the roof on a new garage. His hair was shaggy, crowned with gold. His jeans rode fashionably low and tight. When he turned, he had a smile that dared her to keep looking.

"Why don't you just whistle," he'd called down, smiling that deeply dimpled smile.

She'd refused to blush or look away. She'd been daring that day. Lazily, she'd lifted an arm to shield her eyes from the sun. Her long, straight hair had swept down her back as she'd tilted her chin. She'd given it a shake and walked on.

"Nice view," she'd called, looking over her shoulder. Then it had been his turn to watch.

If he'd felt defensive or self-conscious around her country-club set as their relationship developed, he hadn't shown it. He had the inner strength that allowed him to walk away from petty insults, a quality she hadn't appreciated then. Anyway, she hadn't needed him to impress anyone, she'd wanted him for something else. And oh how he'd wanted her. Marcie shivered at the strength of the memories. Nights and dawns, secret meetings and wet grass.

She stood up, wincing at the way her knee cracked, and went around to the other side of the door to begin a fresh coat of varnish. The whispering bristles of the brush brought to mind her mother's breathy, cultured voice, the way the bed creaked as they'd sat down for a talk. Not the one about sex—Marcie had gotten that at thirteen. This one had been about a different kind of responsibility.

In fact, everyone had done his or her part to make sure she'd gotten the message. She had a position to uphold. Who she was outweighed what she wanted. She was a Courville.

Marcie closed her eyes and set the brush across the can for a moment. When she picked it up again, the handle was sticky. Sighing, she stretched a kink out of her back and inspected the wood. She stood off at an angle to see if there were any places she'd missed, although she knew she'd gone over it thoroughly. Walking slowly over to a plywood tabletop, she poured some turpentine in a pan, worked the liquid through the brush. Washing away stains. It hadn't been so easy with Ray.

"I've got goals," a young girl's voice said into the fading light of a late-summer afternoon on the porch.

He'd been standing at the foot of the stairs. "And I don't? What do you think I've been working for, going to school—"

"Mine don't include dropping out of college—"

"Who asked you to?" His hands had been in his pockets, his fists clenched with self-control. "I only asked you to come back."

The words were spoken forcefully, but quietly enough for her to ignore them while she completed her speech. "They also don't include marrying just now. You've said yourself, your marriage was a mistake. When people are so young—"

"That's no reason this time."

She didn't want to look him in the eye and risk seeing all the pain reflected there, everything he demanded from life and meant to have.

"Give me one reason."

She hadn't even given him that. She'd shrugged, looking off toward the garden, winding an arm around a column. She still remembered the feel of the white painted plaster, so cool, unbending. She'd wanted to be just like it.

Ray had swept a quick, critical glance over those carefully tended lawns, the view of town, the inlaid walk. Craning his neck, he'd stepped back, retreating until the balustrade of the widow's walk appeared, two stories above. Then he brought his eyes down to her. They lingered for a long moment.

"It should've been obvious, right?"

It was a question no one could answer, certainly not the silent girl on the porch, standing there stunned at the emptiness of seeing her plan work.

He hadn't fought it. He'd walked away, head down, shoulders hunched, like a man who'd come a long way only to find the road ended.

"Well, dammit, I *did* have responsibilities," Marcie exclaimed to the empty shop. "It wouldn't have worked. I would have been unhappy and miserable, and one of us would have wanted out sooner or later."

But it wasn't every day a mistake walked into your life and asked to be corrected. She'd done everything within her considerable willpower to get over him. She'd been determined to get on with her life. But ten years of living showed her the cowardice behind the strength. He'd had more power over her than he knew. And she'd run from him.

Sandy cleared her throat, gingerly coming through the door with the leading edge of a varnished strip of trim, holding it away from her sweater. "Still mulling things over?"

"These fumes are making my head spin." The phone rang. A quick glance showed they both had their hands full. "I'll get it." Draping an old cloth over the receiver so her sticky hands wouldn't dirty it, Marcie picked it up. She knew there was no reason why her heart should rattle like a can full of nails. It wasn't as if she expected Ray to call.

She murmured a few hasty replies and hung up. "Court clerk," she announced, "I have to report Monday at eight A.M."

"What are you going to do about Crane?"

"I thought we'd go over how you're going to run the shop yourself."

"We've gone over it. What about Crane?"

Marcie sighed. Best friends had a way of ignoring evasions and getting to the point. "That's what I've been thinking about."

"Obviously."

"I set a goal—"

Sandy rushed in to complete the thought. "And he interfered with the goals you had at the time, so why feel guilty, is that it?"

"Uh-uh. A new goal. I need to find out why he's back in town."

"Sounds reasonable."

"It may be nothing at all."

"Could be."

"Just business."

"Uh-huh."

"I can't kid myself that I'm the only reason he's here, when it's been so long."

"Right-oh."

"Is that all you have to say?"

"Sounds like you're talking yourself into this just fine as it is."

Marcie sighed. "It's just—"

"What?"

That kiss. Why had he kissed her? She touched her fingertips to her lips and inhaled the acrid smell of turpentine. Was that a sign? The growl of the backhoe excavating near the new carports intruded on her thoughts. There was entirely too much digging going on. "All I want to do is get this trial over with."

"And find out why he's back."

She pressed her lips together in a tight line. Maybe it was the way he looked at her, or the way she melted when he did, but Marcie had a sinking feeling she already knew why Ray Crane had come back.

Four

The purposely bland room held all the tension of ten strangers forced to make chitchat. Another juror entered to a silent sigh of relief. Introductions were made again around the walnut table. Marcie ran her fingers along the highly polished veneer. They made a squeak like a small animal in a trap. That fast, Ray's gaze was on her. She curled her fingernails into her palm and put her hands in her lap. She didn't want to show him fear, or awareness, or anything except how she'd changed.

A middle-aged man in a sport coat stood up, a self-satisfied tilt to his grin. Marcie got the impression he was in real estate. Perhaps she'd met him at the club.

"Gentlemen, ladies," his voice was a tad too loud for the small room, though he was the only one not to notice. "I think maybe we ought to get around to choosing a foreman. Or forelady, for those of you of that persuasion." He grinned a salesman's grin. "Gear's the name. My card." He handed out a stack of them. "Just take one and pass 'em along."

Marcie remembered Ray's remark two weeks ago at the shop: At least you didn't hand out business cards. She glanced up at him as she passed the stack. He was grinning, and she knew with a shiver that they shared the joke without speaking.

"Do we make nominations or what?" one woman asked, breaking their silent communication.

"The bailiff may give us some advice on that. Why don't we wait for him?"

"A forewoman might be good, since there are nine women to three men," a young woman suggested.

"Forewoman, forelady?"

"Maybe we should call this foreplay." Ray's remark brought chuckles all around as he joined the line at the coffeepot. He held up a cup in Marcie's direction. She shook her head and mouthed the words "No thanks." When his eyes lingered on her lips, she dismissed it as her imagination.

"For all we know, they could be in there plea bargaining right now," Ray said. "The case might never be tried."

"Good point."

"The man's right."

Is that what he wanted, Marcie wondered, to get back to his business and have no more contact with her? If she could convince herself of that, she might be disappointed but she'd certainly sleep better at night.

She watched him empty a packet of sugar into his cup, then stir it. The polystyrene cup was lost in his large hand. He knocked the wooden stirrer twice against the rim and lifted it, drawing it slowly between his lips as he took his seat. She remembered those lips, their insistence, how they'd felt two weeks ago when he'd kissed her and she hadn't turned away.

"Marcie?"

She liked the way he said her name. Low in his throat, with a gentle gruffness.

"Marcie."

She blinked. "Yes?"

"You're a long-standing member of this community, how about running for foreman?"

"Me?"

The others looked to her in silent support. She made a reasonable alternative to the realtor.

"She had no problem standing up to the judge," someone noted.

"Or speaking out in court. I could never stand up in front of that many people," an older woman remarked, nervously patting her gray hair.

"Then we're decided."

"Here now, we haven't even voted," Mr. Gear said. "We oughta do this right." He began tearing off pages of a small notepad and handing them out. "Write in anyone you want," he added magnanimously.

His company logo was on every page, followed by the name Dick G. Gear. "Should be a landslide," Ray commented wryly. He spelled Courville aloud as he wrote. "That is right, isn't it?"

Marcie nodded.

The slips were passed to the end of the table, where a woman in a heavy homemade cardigan collected them. "Well, I must say, this is our first decision as a jury. It looks like it will be Mrs. Courville."

"Miss," Marcie corrected, avoiding the smile on Ray's face. "Quick work," she muttered as she walked past him, deciding on a cup of coffee after all.

"Might as well get everything you can out of the experience."

She remembered those words in another context, spoken softly, urgently, as he'd coaxed her over the edge.

Marcie sat down once more, stirring her coffee and studying the man across the table.

"Not having second thoughts, are you?"

She smiled but said nothing. She was having second and third and fourth thoughts. She'd lost track of how many times she'd looked back when it came to Ray Crane.

While disjointed conversations started up all around the table, Ray took a sip of his coffee. "Are you mad I got you into this? You seem preoccupied."

"Do I?"

"I think I make you nervous." He smiled, the lines around his hazel eyes becoming more prominent.

He must smile often, Marcie thought, her pulse increasing as she thought of what that smile would do for most women. She'd planned on doing more this morning than sitting across from him with a placid smile on her face, as speechless as a—a virgin. "I'm fine," she insisted.

"You've stirred that coffee for a good three minutes."

"So?"

"You didn't put anything in it, Marcie."

She looked down, stricken. "Maybe it's well blended by now."

"Maybe you didn't put anything in it. I was watching."

She was sure he had been. He hadn't taken his eyes off her yet.

She looked at the rest of the jurors, hoping to join in the conversation, but she couldn't pick up the thread. Some kind of juror she'd make!

The bailiff knocked and entered, counting heads. "Everyone have their juror badges? Good. Sorry about the doughnuts, people. We usually have a dozen set out. See you found the coffee. You'll have to sit in the same seats as when you were chosen. Has anyone forgotten?" The bailiff looked to the diagram on his clipboard.

"Remember?" Ray asked Marcie, his gaze pinning her, the one word filled with meaning.

"Yes." She remembered. So many things.

They heard a gavel pound in the other room. The bailiff held open the door. Ray was behind her as they filed in. She'd have to get used to his hand on her back, the way he took her elbow to escort her up the first step. Ray always did have old-world manners. The kind to help a lady down from a stagecoach, or a pedestal.

The opening arguments against Walter Steinbeck read like a shopping list of criminal activity. Embezzlement, fraud, operating dummy corporations for the purpose of concealing and laundering illegal income. Marcie studied the nondescript middle-aged man sitting at the far table. Neatly dressed in a navy suit with a burgundy tie, he turned a silver cuff link over a few times as the prosecutor outlined his case. Occasionally he picked up a matching silver pen and took notes on a legal pad, the way a high-priced insurance salesman or a seller of pre-owned automobiles would.

Judge Rosen got the jury's attention with a stern look over his reading glasses. "Now, people, you've been given the rules of evidence. Remember again that what the attorneys say in opening and closing arguments are simply their interpretations of the case. They are not fact. The only thing you can consider in weighing your verdict is what is said under oath on this witness stand. Mr. Spannick has presented the prosecution's case, Mr. Hazelton will now outline the case as the defense sees it. If we're lucky, we'll get through this by lunchtime," he added under his breath.

The fascinating process kept Marcie's mind on the trial, as she'd hoped it would. It was a mental challenge, keeping every rule of order in mind, as well as the totally opposing points of view presented by the attorneys. She concentrated fiercely, her gaze directed at the defendant as Mr. Hazelton outlined his record of community service, his education, his sense of responsibility.

One point stuck in Marcie's mind. As a witness, Mrs. Steinbeck wasn't present in the courtroom. Far from supporting her husband, she'd divorced him and would be testifying against him. That was according to the prosecutor, Mr. Spannick. Taking her duty as a juror seriously, Marcie refused to speculate. She brought her attention back to Mr. Hazelton, who was reading aloud from a list of every charity Walter Steinbeck had ever raised funds for, every pancake breakfast he'd ever attended.

Faced with so many details, she could almost

put Ray Crane out of her mind. Except when he turned his head and she caught an occasional whiff of his after-shave. A corner of her mind wanted to know the name of it. Her gaze flicked downward as he crossed his legs in the cramped space; he gave her a quick, pained smile and a wink. By the time she'd subdued a flight of butterflies and fashioned a suitably polite smile, he was looking at the defendant again.

Marcie squirmed in her chair. The morning was beginning to drag. There was a pause as the attorneys shuffled papers and the judge talked to the court reporter. Mr. Hazelton was nearly done, searching in his briefcase for one more piece of paper to present.

For his part, Walter Steinbeck was either a deceiving conniver who'd stolen more than a hundred thousand dollars over five years or a financial manager improperly promoted, given woefully inadequate supervision, who moved money from account to account for purposes which, his defense attorney promised in a dramatic tone, would be revealed in testimony.

"And as you jurors are aware, after hearing Judge Rosen's stirring words, testimony is the only thing that counts. Not flowery opening speeches." Hazelton waved a hand dismissively at his honorable opponent.

As if in agreement, Marcie's stomach grumbled loudly.

Heads as far away as the first row of spectators turned. Ray tugged at his tie with a hooked finger and pursed his lips to hide a smile. Then he winked at Marcie, letting his gaze fall to where her hand sat lightly on her stomach.

She was mortified. Even the judge had heard

it. Ray surreptitiously reached over and patted her knee. His fingers skimmed not only her hem but the silk of her hose. Marcie sat up as if she'd gotten a shot of electric current.

Attention shifted back to the defense attorney digging through his briefcase. "I'm afraid the paper I'd planned to present is back at my office, your honor."

"That doesn't do us much good here, Mr. Hazelton. When do you think you can locate it?" the judge asked.

"During lunch, I'm sure."

"All right then, it's about time we had a break. Bailiff, could you remove the jury? Ladies and gentlemen, be back at one-thirty. I don't abide tardiness."

The jurors sighed as one. Their heads were swimming with points and counterpoints.

"What about lunch?" the realtor asked loudly as the bailiff led them into the jury room. "We didn't get doughnuts this morning, you know." He spoke as if they'd been denied a constitutional right.

"Sorry," the bailiff murmured before addressing the jurors as a group. "For lunch, you're on your own. Anywhere within driving distance. The parking lot gets pretty full at noon with people coming in to pay parking tickets, so you might have a ways to walk when you get back."

"It's not on the court?"

"Only if the judge orders you to stay in for deliberations."

"Do we have to eat together?" someone else asked.

"No. However, if you do, be sure not to discuss the case."

Ray stepped in behind Marcie as the jurors filed out.

"I think we can manage that," he said, his breath brushing her cheek as he leaned over her shoulder. His hand rested lightly on her lower back.

Marcie was glad she had a thick wool coat on. Maybe she was only imagining the pressure.

"We have a lot to catch up on."

"Yes, we do." Why he'd kissed her, for one. Why she'd let him go.

"How about if I take you someplace we've never been before?"

Suggestiveness. If it wasn't in his tone that meant it was all in her mind—and under her skin, pulsing and shimmering. The soft whoosh of the door closing behind them was like the breath leaving her lungs. She had to consciously loosen the grip on her purse. "Lead the way."

"Don't I always?"

Damn that smile.

The place he chose for lunch was a long, narrow room strung with hanging plants. Black and white tiles decorated the floor, imitating the checked tablecloths, and the walls were white-washed brick. Each and every waitress wore a black turtleneck, a white jacket, and a name tag that read *Fern*. It was Fern's Bar.

Marcie waved gaily to the owner. In the space of five minutes three friends stopped by to chat. Her smile was brilliant, her manner easy and at home.

Before Ray could envy them, she flashed a smile his way, her eyes twinkling. She had a way of looking directly into his eyes that made him think she was about to confide some magical secret.

"I've been here before."

"So I noticed. I thought the place was new."

"It is, only the customers are old! Old friends, that is."

She paused, waiting for his response, her smile riding on whether or not he smiled.

She had a way of tying his stomach in knots. Even after all the years. He swore up and down it was all a matter of social polish. Heck, he watched her in action right there in the restaurant. The sorry fact was, he could watch her for the rest of his life and never tire of her. And never learn lesson one: You don't fall in love with a woman simply because she gazes into your eyes.

He knew he should listen to his head, not his heart. And definitely not that part of him that turned to quivering, pulsing fire just because she reached across the table, touched his hand lightly, and said, "Let's order."

"Let's," he croaked.

"You sound like you could use some water."

Among other things. He swallowed a glassful in one gulp. He could have emptied the carafe. "Think we can go over this in an hour?"

Marcie opened the greeting card that served as a menu. "Depends on how deeply you want to get into it."

Deep. He hooked his finger in the knot of his tie and tugged, toying with the navy-blue silk as he picked out his burger. Leaning back, his knees bumped hers. He kept them there.

She was studying the checks in the tablecloth, shoulders set in that effortless way, head level enough to balance a book on.

"I heard about your divorce."

"Six years ago." She smiled. They could've been discussing the weather.

"No kids?"

She shook her head. This territory wasn't so rocky after all. A lot had happened in the intervening years; she'd grown up a lot.

"How was he?" Ray asked bluntly.

Marcie gulped her own water, her heart turning over with a thump. She set down the glass silently. "How do you mean?"

He shrugged. "Was he a womanizer, a drinker?"

"Nothing that dramatic, I'm afraid."

"Not enough in common?"

She smiled again, curious at the way he clenched his jaw each time she did. She could make this so much easier for them both, put them at ease. "Just the opposite. No spice, no discoveries. We were taking each other for granted within a year. I couldn't see spending the rest of my life being so . . ."

"So . . .?"

"So sedate, sedated." Marcie caught herself. She'd never said an unkind word about her ex. In fact, she prided herself on the civility of their divorce. She looked at Ray. Being around this man was never easy. The word *unsettling* came to mind. "Maybe that makes no sense."

He squinted as the front door opened and a shaft of light cut through the room. The lines etched deeper around his eyes. "I can't imagine life with you being dull."

The wry smile he turned on her had her heart bumping her ribs. Why didn't he come right out and say it? *If I'd been the one you married, it wouldn't have been.*

Marcie placed a paper napkin in her lap as precisely as if she were dining with the queen. Under the table her hand trembled. "You haven't remarried?"

He shook his head, hand-combing strands of hair off his forehead. Marcie clutched the napkin. It made a rustling, whispering sound, tickled her palm—unlike his hair, which had always been thick, straight, a little too long. Unmanageable. Misbehaving.

"I'm surprised you remember the first one," he said.

"Her name was Carol." *I remember, Ray. More than you know.*

"She's remarried. Happily. Funny how mistakes can correct themselves, if the right person comes along."

For once she looked away. She'd stopped clutching the napkin, her fingers darted from black to white squares on the tablecloth. Ray covered them with his hand. She didn't withdraw. Slowly, she brought her gaze back to his face.

"Coffee, folks?" Fern asked as she set two salads on the table.

"Thanks." Ray held out his cup.

"I'd like iced tea," Marcie said.

Fern reached into a bucket with a pair of tongs, then plopped two cubes into Marcie's glass. The third got away, sliding across the table like a roll of the dice. Ray caught it, licking the cool wetness off his fingertips.

The shock of memory hit, Marcie's stomach lurched like an elevator on a downward plunge. On a humid summer night he'd plucked an ice cube out of a tall, sweaty glass and ran it down her throat, a wet, melting trail raising and puckering and numbing her nipples until he sucked them warm again.

She cleared her throat, took a sip of tea, and cleared it again. What was she doing? This was supposed to be an easy, get-acquainted lunch. She was trying to find a socially acceptable way for them to sit comfortably side by side for another week in that courtroom. If that meant getting to the point, so be it; she'd swallow her pride as soon as she swallowed the piece of lettuce from her salad. "I've been wanting to ask why you've come back."

"Ask."

It galled her that the one question that came to mind was *Why did you kiss me?*

"You said you were building a mall."

"That's what I said."

"Is that all?"

"Are you asking why I didn't come back earlier?" Hazel eyes could be surprisingly steely.

"If you don't wish to get into this, that's fine with me." It would be a relief, in fact.

"Just let it go, is that it, Marcie?" The way she'd let him go?

She didn't want him to go, she knew it, sensed it. She felt hotter, colder, tinglier, more everything just sitting across from him. Her pulse drummed a syncopated beat every time she caught him studying her. She'd felt faint and giddy all morning. Lack of food had nothing to do with it. Appetite did.

Her emotions were as checkered as the tablecloth. It was like a chess game with too many choices, a dozen ways to jump, none of them quite so black and white. "It's been a long time for us. The past may not be pertinent to the people we are now."

"Pertinent." He grumbled over her two-dollar word, downing his coffee just in time to hold out his cup to a passing waitress. "Leaded."

"We can't talk about the trial."

"No."

"We've both started businesses," Marcie suggested. "We could talk about that."

"Hiring and billables?" He grimaced and patted his pockets for a roll of antacids. The burger hadn't arrived and he hated salad.

"Payables?" she shrugged and laughed. They were back on neutral ground.

Until he popped an antacid in his mouth and pinned her with a look. "How about outstanding debts?"

She tensed ever so subtly but didn't run. He gave her credit for that.

"Are you suggesting we owe each other something?"

"Forget I said it." He shook it off and downed his coffee. It didn't matter if once upon a time she'd used him. He'd been younger then, more gullible. It was the woman he was interested in now, although interested was too mild a term. Watching another shaft of light glitter across her hair, he felt warmth he didn't want to feel spreading in his lower body. "There's no point looking back."

"I agree."

So why couldn't he stop looking? Because she was still the most beautiful woman he'd ever known. Because he wanted her, always had and always would. Because the knowledge that he'd once had her and had walked away ate at him. A hundred antacids wouldn't cure that. "We couldn't go back if we tried."

Her smile was like a shaft of light, it cut through him. "I'm very relieved you think that way. Young people make so many mistakes, they go overboard—"

"They make out like there's no tomorrow."

She laughed again. He didn't miss it when she touched his hand, quickly, congratulating him on making a joke.

"Adults can do that too, Marcie."

"Speaking from experience?"

"I was always the one with experience."

She pursed her lips and gave him a scolding grin. "I thought we were putting this behind us."

"So we can start fresh." He took her hand deliberately in his, watching the heat rise in her cheeks. "What would you say to dinner someplace more private? My place."

"No!" Startled, the word escaped her before she could qualify it with a few polite phrases.

"That's direct, at least." He laughed dryly.

"With the trial I'll be very busy at night."

"I could give to the cause." He grinned. Appealing, disarming, threateningly seductive.

She withdrew her hand with a jerk. "There's the business and Mother to visit and the construction to oversee."

Ray leaned back and glanced at his Rolex. "Keep going. I want to see how many excuses you can come up with in sixty seconds."

"You have a business too," she hurried on, "or are they doing so well they don't need you?"

"Did you ever love me?" The question hovered over them like one of the slowly twirling fans. He hadn't known he was going to ask, he only knew it had been too long coming. "Tell me no and I'll take a hike."

She stared at him. Love him? She'd been all over him, an uninhibited wanton at his beck and call.

"Not that it matters," he said gruffly, tearing apart a dinner roll. "The past is past."

Even iced tea couldn't ease the ache in her throat. In her carefully organized life she didn't ride roller coasters, recalling memories only to dismiss them as if they'd never mattered. Perhaps to Ray they hadn't. Perhaps she should keep that in mind.

"Better off forgotten," he said, more to the roll than her.

She squared her shoulders. "It certainly is."

"Think we'll do any better this time around?"

A puppet, that's what she was, her strings pulled taut, then dropped. She wasn't about to be played this way. "There won't be a this time, Ray."

"Don't think so?"

"I know so. Now if you'll excuse me." She placed a tightly wadded napkin on the table and marched to the ladies room.

They'd eaten in relative silence, leaving half their food on their plates. After paying the check, Ray took her elbow and steered her out the door. She was perfectly capable of walking on her own, but she knew better than to argue.

She tripped off the curb. All right, so she couldn't walk and examine the outline of his jaw out of the corner of her eye at the same time. "Sorry."

"What *are* you comfortable talking about?" he asked out of the blue.

"Do we have to talk?"

"Yes," he practically hissed. Another antacid was ground to chalky powder between his teeth.

Marcie picked her way carefully across the brick street. "I don't know what we have in common."

"How about sex?" He came to a halt in the crosswalk.

She scowled and continued on without him.

"We did have something special, Marcie. Or is that a cliché?"

"Would you mind not yelling it after me on a public street?"

"You won't meet me in private. Although, as I recall, you liked secret meetings. It added to the thrill. Exactly what your marriage lacked."

She walked on, hands deep in her pockets, head down against a brisk wind. She felt hairs dancing on the back of her neck and told herself it had nothing to do with Ray coming up behind her.

How about sex, indeed! Stalking up the courthouse steps, Marcie was so furious, she couldn't even remember what she'd eaten for lunch. Ray Crane undermined her resolve, disrupted her emotions, embarrassed her in public, and delighted in doing it! Worst of all, he made her want things a sane, sensible woman had no business wanting.

"Not this time, Ray. I won't let you do this to me."

It would have made a good rallying cry, except she was directing it at the wrong person. Ray wasn't the one on the verge of losing control, swooning over a simple kiss.

He'd overwhelmed a girl a lifetime ago with his blunt, seductive ways. All too willingly, Marcie added with scrupulous fairness. But Marcie wasn't that girl anymore. If she prided herself on controlling her life, there was only one surefire way of convincing them both of that fact.

She'd kiss him back. And she wouldn't lose control.

Five

The pistol shot of a gavel ended the first day's session. The jury cleared out quickly to a chorus of *See you tomorrow*s.

Waiting in line at the coatrack, Ray reached over Marcie and seized hers. "Let me."

She silently congratulated him on the maneuver. She couldn't leave until she came to him. She'd thought once she could handle him. She'd been the one handled, expertly. But not this time. Remembering her new resolve, she stepped comfortably into his arms. "Thank you."

They were the last two people in the room. His hands rested on her shoulders. *Now or never, Marcie.* She took a deep, unsteady breath and turned to him. It gave her a small measure of power to see the way his eyes darkened when she looked up at him. She stepped closer.

He tensed, like a panther sniffing the wind, making sure before abandoning his cover.

"I thought you wanted to talk about sex." She was playing with fire. A tiny, unprotected part of her heart made peace with the fact she might never know if he'd loved her before. But she had to know, now, if the woman could do things the girl couldn't, such as kiss Ray Crane and walk away unburned.

She stepped forward until the front of her coat brushed his suit jacket. She was conscious of the slightly waxy smell of closely shaved skin and cologne, the shirt smell of starch and cotton and soap.

He lifted his chin, drawing her eyes to his throat. He hadn't answered.

"Nervous? Not you, Ray." She touched him, trailing fingertips along a lapel, letting them stray onto his shirt, picking up hints of the heat within. "You no more belong in a suit than a wild stallion belongs in a saddle," she teased, just giving him the barest of smiles.

"You don't think so?" He squared his shoulders defensively.

She tugged at the knot in his tie, drawing it downward until one end came loose. "I will admit you've accommodated nicely. A person who'd just met you would think you were born to it."

"You remember differently."

"I think we remember a lot of things differently. That may be our problem."

"Then we're not talking about sex." He ran a finger down her cheek. "You remember as well as I do. That's why you run."

Was that also why her eyes fluttered closed every time he touched her? She opened them through sheer willpower. He was challenging her, his voice husky, grating, and low. She wasn't running this time. He was taut as a bowstring; she could bend or break him.

"How do you remember me, Marcie?"

"Barebacked," she said in a breathy voice.

His teeth clenched, unclenched. A hand fumbled through her hair, gripping her head to steady it. "I could still take you for quite a ride."

"Try it."

On the edge he paused, testing the waters before he committed himself. "I want you to want it."

She smiled wider this time, her lips parted, and she released a puff of laughter as her breath mingled with his. "What do you think I'm doing here?"

"I hope to God you know," he said with a groan, crushing her against him.

Mouths sought open mouths, willing tongues. He pierced her with each kiss, changing, deepening, retreating and repositioning but never withdrawing. His other hand splayed on her lower back, angling downward, finding a muscle that tensed at his touch, released, and tensed again.

She felt it. She wanted it. But it distracted her. She wanted to concentrate on him, how high she had to reach to coil her arms around his neck. But she was intent; there was skin, heat, the prickly abrasion of the faint stubble along the edge of his jaw, the opening in his collar. Yes, that's what she'd been seeking, an opening. She pressed her mouth to the hollow at the base of his throat and heard him moan. Yes, she was in control, she was choosing to do this, the weakness in her legs was her decision, the melting flow was not a surrender.

Keep your head, a voice warned. *Touch me there,* another pleaded. Flares of anticipation flooded through her. Things were spinning so fast during the small eternity of each kiss that she could almost forget she was supposed to be in charge.

This is what she wanted—Ray.

Their bodies bucked as he hooked a chair leg with his ankle and dragged it out of the way. He pressed her back, and she felt the sharp angle of the jury table against her derriere. His body was flush against hers, the wool of his suit coat was clutched in her fingers. "Ray."

There was no way to hide what she was doing to him, it was obvious between them, a hard ache matched by harsh shallow breaths, a low moan of guttural surrender when he tore his mouth from hers and held her face trapped between his hands.

"Marcie!" His voice was a harsh croak, her name a blunt demand. The smell of her perfume dizzied him, the waft of body heat inside the satin lining of her white winter coat made him break out in a sweat. This damn suit. He had too many clothes on, so did she.

The champagne-colored lining played off her hair. Her blue eyes were ice glittering with fire. Her lids were hot when he kissed them, her mouth open and wet. Her hair was disheveled, but still held by too many pins. She wore it tied up, he thought. He was the man to untie her, the only one.

He put his hands on her waist and lifted until she was sitting on the table.

Her eyes widened. With a nudge from his knee, her legs parted.

"Don't stop me, Marcie."

"Here?"

He knew that look. She was shocked. She was

thrilled. With him she'd dare anything. No woman had ever given him that rush of power, that jolt of pure adrenaline. "Just do it. With me."

One large palm was flat against her back, scooting her toward him. His other was on her thigh, under her skirt, abrading her stockings with a raspy sound, searching higher until he found the bump of a garter. He swallowed hard. "Tell me the only thing in my way is lace."

Marcie's heartbeat thundered in her ears as doubts swirled like a whirlpool in her head. But all sounds were drowned out by his voice, filled with desperate need. He couldn't look at her, not if he wanted to maintain control. Control. The word flitted in and out of her thoughts like so much confetti.

She ran a hand down his shirtfront, her fingertips on the warmed metal of his belt buckle. They couldn't, not there. And yet, there was no stopping. How could you stop what was never meant to be controlled? Rational decisions and sheer, overpowering instinct didn't mix, didn't stand a chance.

"Ahem!"

It took a minute for the sound to penetrate, for his hands to freeze.

"I'll be locking up the jury room now." The bailiff flipped a piece of paper over his clipboard, studying it as if he'd find further instructions there.

Ray stepped back, creating a barrier behind which Marcie could snap her legs closed. When all the tuckings of skirt and blouse were done, he wordlessly lifted her off the table. But he didn't let her go. Between him and the table edge there was no space to escape. He petted her hair, making her look into his eyes once more. What she saw there belied his tender gesture. They were far from finished, he wanted her to know that. His body and hers left no room for doubt.

He glanced over his shoulder to the bailiff. "We'll get out of here."

"Eight A.M. tomorrow."

Marcie could almost hear the smile in his voice.

Ray's was solemn in comparison. "We'll be here." He held out his arm.

The blood rushing to Marcie's cheeks was at war with the excitement pooling elsewhere. She was dizzy, almost nauseated, and her equilibrium had gone completely haywire. She should be ashamed, mortified. As clearheadedness returned, she was. It was the keen, lingering disappointment that surprised her, over the fact they'd been interrupted.

So much for turning the tables! she thought. So much for staying in control! If it hadn't stopped when it did, if that man had come in ten minutes later . . . it didn't bear thinking about.

Ray worked the buttons of his suit coat as they hit a brisk March wind. Marcie didn't bother, her fingers were shaking too hard. She wrapped her coat tightly closed, one hand clenched at the collar.

"I'll take you to your car," Ray said. "Then I'll follow you home."

She stopped, snow falling around them as they stood in the orange pool of a streetlight. It was barely dusk. The lamp buzzed overhead like the rush of blood in her ears. Marcie took a deep breath but couldn't calm a galloping heart. "What I did back there—"

"What we did," he insisted tensely.

Her eyes flared. He was stubborn. How could she have forgotten that? Apparently she'd forgotten a lot of negative qualities about Ray Crane. His drive, his absolute shamelessness. The man would do anything, and he didn't seem to care who knew it. He had no sense of decorum whatsoever. "What *you* did, I might add."

His smile was slanted, his tone just this side of derisive. "You're claiming I took advantage of you?"

"You think you know exactly what you're doing, don't you?"

"Once upon a time you led me to believe I was an expert. Not that you had anyone to compare me with."

He followed her as she marched across the lot. The county employees had gone home, all the court sessions had let out. The only cars remaining were for the night shift at the jail.

"Are you going to claim this was some kind of fluke?"

"You kissed me hello, I thought I'd kiss you back. For old times' sake." It was close enough to the truth, but it rang as hollow as his laugh.

"Old times' sake? Marcie."

She kept marching.

"Marcie!" He grabbed her arm. She skidded to a stop on the icy pavement. "A kiss on the cheek is for old times' sake. If the way you acted just now is your way of renewing an old acquaintance, I'd hate to see you at a high school reunion."

That did it! She rounded on him, hand raised. But the motion was too sudden on the slick snow. Her foot shot out from under her, and he had to catch her to save her from falling. They stood there, breathing hard, eyes alight. Puffs of fog darted between them.

"How dare you!"

"I could say the same. You want to lie about what just happened? Why not lie about all of it? Why not say we never had anything?"

"I never act that way, never."

"Except with me."

She couldn't deny it, not and make him believe it. They both knew it too well. He was the man who made her drop her defenses, cast aside inhibitions bred into her from birth. He was also the only man who had ever made her want to turn and run.

It took everything she had but she managed to keep her voice level. "I don't want this, Ray."

"If I came to you in the night, would you turn me away?"

Her eyes flashed again. She wasn't sure which of them she was angrier with. "Don't bank on it." She unlocked her car door and swung it open.

With one flat palm he slammed it shut. "You're not leaving until you tell me why you went so far."

"You took me by surprise."

"So did you. Do you always touch men that way when you're just being friendly?"

"I loosened your tie, for heaven's sake!"

"And kissed me damn good."

"Hush!"

The mood crackled, Ray's face creased into a smile. "Not in public. I should have known. You don't want to be seen with me. What would people say?"

"Don't you dare mock me. That's not it and you know it."

At the other end of the lot, a car door shut.

They both turned. A policeman sat in his marked car, patiently watching them.

"He thinks I'm accosting you," Ray said.

"You are."

"Don't tell me you were buying me off with one last quickie?"

She turned fast enough to hide the tears. The air was cold, her eyes stung. "I don't believe in humiliating myself. That's what we almost did back there."

"So we pick a better spot next time."

"And get it over with?" She laughed bitterly and opened her car door. He didn't stop her this time.

"You make me crazy, Marcie. Hungry. I've never stopped wanting you." There, he'd said it.

The engine roared to life. His wanting her hadn't stopped her leaving the last time, why should it now? He muttered an ugly curse directed at himself. She was in such a hurry to leave, she flattened the pedal to the floor. He jumped out of the way as she swung the car out of the lot, windows still steamed.

The police car pulled out a few seconds later, tires whispering through the slush.

Ray found his tie wadded in his pocket and flung it on the floor after his suit coat. He sidestepped packing boxes on his way to the wet bar. Grinding off the gold foil of an imported beer, he flipped off the cap. The house was chilly and damp, barely moved into. He was looking for something more permanent. Now he wasn't so sure. Derby might be a sensible site for Crane Corporation headquarters, but it was Marcie's home.

He strode across the nondescript living room,

irritated as always at the lack of trim, personality, or character in the newly built model. He'd gotten it through a builder friend who wasn't intimidated by the competition. Houses weren't Crane's market and never would be. A good apartment, a nice condo would do for him. He'd show off in the office complex arena and leave house building to others.

Not that any of it mattered if he couldn't get Marcie to so much as look at him.

In the bathroom he twisted the shower nozzle, steam rose from the scalding water. The water heater kicked on with a clunk somewhere in the basement. He'd better hurry, or he'd be standing in cold water by the time his usual twenty-minute shower was done. The beer bottle was dotted with moisture when Ray's shirt hit the floor. He stripped off his socks, stepped out of his pants, and closed the glass door, bracing for the pummeling hot water.

It wasn't enough to distract him from the physical ache that had yet to subside. Now that he'd had a taste of her, a touch, he'd never get her out of his system.

The soap slipped out of his grasp. He cursed and fumbled on the shower floor for it, bumping his head on the way back up. He smacked his palm against the tiled walls, wondering how long his cheek would have stung if she'd succeeded in slapping him. He smiled grimly. "It's the thought that counts."

Spreading his hands against the tile, he let the water beat down. If *his* thoughts counted for anything, he and Marcie would be in bed by now. She'd be telling him she loved him, she wanted him, she always had. "Dream on, bud."

Instead she avoided him, asked him to leave, reacted only to his touch, their whispers, the sexual excitement the two of them generated. He could get close to her body, but not her heart. Not ten years before, not now.

That thought stung. A half bottle of beer waited for him on the counter. He knew one wasn't going to be nearly enough.

She arrived at seven fifty-five A.M., five minutes before the bailiff came in to count them. Her cheeks were bright pink. Ray wondered how many times she'd walked around the parking lot before getting up the courage to come in.

She nodded to the other jurors but didn't look at him. Not even when they filed into the courtroom. Her only reaction was the start she gave when he touched her arm, helping her up the first step of the jury box. He kept his distance after that. In the closely set chairs, it wasn't easy.

It took a few moments for everyone to file in. But it was enough time for Ray to calculate the damage done by last night.

She was wearing a power suit, charcoal gray with a faint stripe. Her satin blouse was antique white, like her skin in some lights. Ray knew a suit of armor when he saw one.

Her nails were polished a light pink. They matched her lipstick. He boldly reached over and closed his hand over hers. Her eyes darted immediately to his. His thumb brushed the shiny pink surface of her fingertips. "For someone who works with wood, you keep your hands very soft. Who is it for?"

She withdrew, hands folded tightly in her lap.

With effort, she kept her voice light. "You were expecting calluses?"

"I never expect less than perfection from you." With that he looked away.

Marcie wished the court would come to order so she could think of something beside his cryptic comment. Perfection? She smiled wryly to herself and wondered how many other people would consider that an insult. Perhaps she'd heard the phrase *ice princess* one too many times, subtle hints from Sandy that she should lighten up. But the night before hadn't been the answer. The night before had been a disaster, a complete failure, nothing short of the collapse of her pretense at self-control.

And it was all his fault.

Marcie watched Walter Steinbeck and his attorney, Mr. Hazelton, enter. She was partly to blame for what had happened, if not entirely at fault. So how would she deal with Ray Crane from now on? Give him the cold shoulder? An ice princess idea.

Court was called to session and Judge Rosen entered. Marcie exhaled slowly, rescued temporarily from her tortured thoughts and even more twisted feelings.

"I'd like to call Mr. George Weidman of the accounting firm of Hardiman, Weidman, and Crowley." The prosecution began its second full day with a mind-numbing explanation of fundamental business accounting and the procedures used by Walter Steinbeck's firm.

After lunch, the jurors settled in for the afternoon. Marcie was still swallowing the aftertaste of the peanut-butter sandwich she'd wolfed down at the shop. She'd breezed in, claiming she wanted to touch base.

"You've only been gone one and a half days," Sandy noted wryly. "I think I've handled it so far."

"It's still my responsibility. Tell me who's called."

Over coffee and that dry sandwich they'd gone over every outstanding account. That used up ten minutes.

"Is there another reason you want to be here?" Sandy asked ingenuously.

"They were talking accounting all morning. It gave me a wonderful craving to go over our own books."

"And?"

She shrugged. "Where else would I go for lunch?"

"Restaurants are usually a good bet."

"You can keep the sarcasm. Besides," Marcie raised her cup to her lips, "where else can I get coffee like this?" She gulped and made a face. "What is this? It tastes like used motor oil."

"It's Turkish."

"You haven't served it to customers, have you?"

"The only ones we've had know better than to ask. So tell me, how's the enforced togetherness working with Ray Crane?"

Marcie shot a glance at her watch. "Gotta get going."

Sandy's brows rose. "So soon?"

"The judge will have me locked up if I'm late."

"In that case, maybe I should drug your coffee. Then I could take over the company for good."

"On the one hand, I wouldn't drink enough of your coffee to be drugged." Marcie smiled as she slipped into her coat, the satin-lined whisperings bringing back memories of the night before. She promptly forgot whatever the other hand was.

"I've got enough on my mind without office intrigues."

"Especially when courtroom intrigues are so much more interesting," Sandy murmured as Marcie headed out the door.

Back in the courtroom, Marcie fought down her irritation. Since founding Designs on the Past all her energies had gone into the company; she'd barely dated. How could Sandy know this man was any different? To someone who cultivated a certain amount of emotional reserve, the thought that she was so transparent was unnerving. It was one thing to be vulnerable around one's friends, another entirely with a man like Ray Crane.

Six

Mr. Spannick, the prosecutor, waved a computer disk under their noses. Marcie snapped to attention. "For your inspection, ladies and gentlemen. Mr. Weidman, is this one of the diskettes used at the Halliwell Corporation?"

"I believe so," Weidman replied. "I wouldn't be able to say for certain until you called it up."

A small computer was set up on a central table. The prosecutor inserted the diskette. After a few beeps and whirrs, a spreadsheet appeared on the screen.

"This is a little different from the days when two sets of ledger books were used to manage bogus accounts," he explained. "It's all done with computers now. Mr. Weidman, what did Walter Steinbeck say when you confronted him with this diskette and the accounts he'd created on it?"

Hazelton was on his feet. "Objection, Your Honor. It hasn't been established who created those accounts."

"Sustained. Mr. Spannick, would you like to reword—?"

"Mr. Weidman, in the process of your audit, what did Walter Steinbeck say when you confronted him with this diskette?"

"I told him I was removing the diskette from the premises due to accounting irregularities I'd found on it. He told me I couldn't."

"Why?"

"He said it was necessary for his work."

"And what did you suggest?"

"That a copy be made of the diskette. He volunteered to make one himself, overnight, and get it to me the next day."

"You refused?"

"As part of the auditing procedures, I had to refuse. Diskettes can be erased, changed, and often there's no way to discover what information has been removed."

"And when you insisted on taking the original diskette?"

"I'm afraid he begged me."

"He what?"

Mr. Weidman cleared his throat and leaned toward the microphone. "He begged me not to take it. He said what he was working on was only partially finished, and he would miss some sort of deadline if I took the data. When I again offered to copy the diskette there, in his presence, he offered me ten thousand dollars."

"A bribe."

"Yes, that's how I understood it."

"That's all, Your Honor."

Ray sat up a little straighter, tugging on his suit coat. Despite her concentration on the case, Marcie was constantly aware of the little movements he made, the way he slouched to get comfortable, curving his fingers over his pocket, hooking a thumb in his belt. His knees were right up to the railing, his legs were so long. She could still feel the muscles bunched and pressed to hers.

Thankfully Hazelton distracted her, unfolding himself slowly, theatrically from his chair. How would he counter Weidman's damning disclosures? He patted his tie flat against his chest, stroked his chin as he turned over a few pieces of paper, grinning to himself as if he had some information the poor misled jurors did not.

The judge interrupted. "I'm sorry, Mr. Hazelton, I'm not sure we'll have time for this today. Would you like to take it up first thing in the morning?"

His dramatic entrance foiled, Hazelton pursed his lips, eyeing the witness with scorn. "I sincerely hope we can get some more intelligible answers from the witness in the morning. I don't know about the jurors, but his lecture on computerized transfer of funds had my head spinning. Accounting seems to have almost as much double-talk as the computer business. Now that the two are linked, we may never hear an honest word spoken in a courtroom again."

"Thank you for the editorial comment," the judge grumbled. "Opening arguments were yesterday. I take it you'll rest till morning?"

"We will, Your Honor."

The judge banged his gavel. "Eight A.M. tomorrow, people."

There wasn't a morning for the rest of the week when Marcie arrived earlier than seven fifty-five, Ray counted. At lunch she either went to her shop or ate with the other jurors. She was avoiding him with everything she had.

But Ray knew Marcie. What he had planned might be damned near unforgivable in her eyes, but there was no way she'd have it out with him in front of other people. That's why he confronted her by the coatrack on Friday afternoon as the jurors were leaving. "Are you going to go on like this? Pretending I don't exist?"

No heads turned. They didn't have to. As jurors, they were becoming adept at listening.

"We have nothing more to talk about," Marcie said, soft and low. In control.

"I want to talk about what happened the other night."

What had been a hasty weekend exodus among the other jurors turned into a slow retreat.

It wasn't kind of him, but Ray had had four days to confront his feelings, to add up the stakes, to weigh the gamble. And four nights of thoughts of her setting him on fire. He was in no mood to play it safe. He had to get her alone, it was the only way they'd ever learned to communicate. "We talk here, or we find some place private."

Painfully aware of the people surrounding them, Marcie glared at him. He was manipulating her, and she wanted him to know that she knew it. It wouldn't work. There was no way he'd win her over like this. Armed with anger, Marcie faced him down. "You could stop by the shop."

"When?"

"Whenever you feel like it, Mr. Crane. We're open to the public." Stepping through the press of jurors, she let the door swing shut behind her.

In a few minutes, Ray was alone. He didn't crow. He didn't celebrate. For a moment he was too tired to even plan. He was fighting to win her back, the way he should have ten years before. This time, there'd be no sneaking around, no midnight meetings. He had one thing on his side: He'd play by any rules. Lucky for him, no one ever said love was fair.

Marcie had almost talked herself into believing all that accounting talk was the reason she was ankle deep in her company's books. She was becoming too easy a liar. If the man wanted to talk, he could talk. She should be able to handle it. She hoped.

Wasn't that her strategy before? But things happened too fast.

Wasn't that always the way with Ray? Wasn't it his intensity matched with hers that she feared?

She'd think it over. It was Sunday night. Six days had gone by since their infamous scene in the jury room. Her cheeks still colored at the memory of what she'd almost done. It was definitely Ray Crane's fault.

"Mind if I come in?"

She almost jumped out of her skin. Blast. If that's the way she reacted to his voice, what hope did she have of handling his touch?

He ducked his head as he came through the door, swiping a sand-colored lock of hair off his forehead. He smiled.

Marcie kept an eye on her books. She was burning the midnight oil; it was the only way she could exhaust herself into sleep lately. Otherwise dreams of Ray . . . "It's a little late."

"Not too late, I hope."

Marcie bristled at the meaning of his words.

Sandy came bustling out of the side office, a cup of fresh brewed coffee in each hand. "I might as well join you if you insist on working yourself to death like this. This ought to be strong enough to keep us up half the night. Oh." She set down the saucers, switching gears effortlessly. "Or perhaps two cups is just right. Maybe I won't stay after all."

Despite her suggestion, Sandy was clearly offering to play chaperon. It was up to Marcie to refuse or accept. She knew she was tripping over her own pride, but all her life she'd handled things in what she hoped was a levelheaded and mature way. She couldn't exactly ask for help now. This was her battle to fight. Question was, did winning mean getting Ray to leave or stay? "I've kept you late enough, Sandy. Thanks for all your help."

Marcie's rapidly beating heart took over when the sound of Sandy's car engine faded in the distance. Ray stayed on the far side of the room, prowling as he had that first day. His glance darted up the rough planks of the staircase. "Mind if I look?"

Marcie shook her head. As he ascended, she glanced quickly in a mirror. Her opinion ping-ponged between horror at her lack of makeup and pleasure that she hadn't gone to any trouble "just in case" he stopped by. She pulled her hair back into a ponytail, strapped on a handy rubber band, and followed him up.

"Still the old carriage house up here. Some storage space."

A few pieces of straw were scattered across the unpainted wood floor. Ray rolled one under his shoe. "It's a wonder you never got splinters."

Marcie cleared her throat, ignoring his reference. "I believe I owe you an apology." She owed him much more than that.

"For?"

"For almost slapping you last week. I *never* do that. I can't believe what comes over me—" *When I'm around you.*

He grunted, not meeting her gaze. "You've got a temper, when you show it."

That sounded like a reprimand. Marcie let it pass.

He was looking at the old harnesses hanging from the rafters, horseshoes nailed to the beams. He crouched down, sitting on his heels, and scraped together a pile of straw in the corner under a small, dirty window. "Couldn't make much of a bed out of this, could we?"

"Ray."

"Amazing how smell brings back memories."

"I know." She knew every time she sat beside him on the jury, inhaling his cologne. The pictures his aroma evoked were like continual small shocks—they kept her alert, on edge, always aware of him.

Ray inhaled slowly, his heart beating slower, a low thud like a horse's hooves. At least she'd agreed with him on this one thing. He could almost smell the diesel from the gardener's tractor below, hear the rustling of pigeons above, see Marcie at nineteen, peeling off her blouse in the moonlight.

"Does the place look smaller?" she asked. "I've found, when I go back to old places—"

He shook his head, gruffly clearing his throat. "Emptier, maybe. No bales of hay." He glanced at the window. "Dingier."

"Oh, no," she replied instantly, then caught

herself. For some reason she couldn't explain, she didn't want him making it dingy.

"The sound's different," he added, standing up. He stepped toward her slowly, the thump of his heels underlining his words.

"How do you mean?" Standing at the top of the stairs, she couldn't back up without backing down.

"Voices are different. We almost echo." He took another step toward her, gently gripping her elbow in his hand, tugging her away from the stairway. "I remember this place with whispers and soft words. But words always sound different in the dark. Sometimes I even wonder if they mean the same thing."

"The light's always good in here," Marcie added hurriedly, unnecessarily. She walked across to the window. "It'd make a good showplace for wallpapers, that's something else we're thinking of getting into. Or a cute loft."

"I don't think what we got up to here would qualify as cute, Marce."

She flinched. He was intent on making her remember as he closed the distance between them.

"Come here often?" he murmured.

It was a joke, their joke, born of a dozen clandestine meetings. It referred to a river bank, the woods, the high hedges that ringed the west garden. And here.

He ran his hands up and down her arms. Marcie inhaled, short, shallow breaths, each one rich in his scent—male, musky, tangy, reality.

"You took off your blouse. It was our first time," he said hoarsely, the mint of his breath against her cheek another reminder: straw and wintergreen and the damp stable.

"You touched me. It was the first time you'd touched a man."

She remembered. The sound of a lowered zipper, the clink of an unbuckled belt. They'd stood naked while he'd let her study him. Then he'd brought her hands to his body. "Go ahead, touch me."

She'd spent a lot of time on his face, working up the nerve to explore his shoulders and chest, feeling the nipples pebble under her fingers, the hair curl and spring back. She'd even dared his waist, the tops of his thighs. But it was his hand on hers that led her back to the center. Her persistent teacher.

The shock of that smooth skin, stretched and hard and pulsing with need for her, made the palm of her hand itch.

"Marcie," he'd chided after a moment, "are we just going to shake hands?"

She'd giggled, he'd laughed. She'd never known men and women laughed at a time like that, or other times.

It wasn't until later, much later, that she'd found herself groping for him in the dark, inarticulate cries begging with stunning eagerness for more. Suddenly she'd needed no instruction, astonishing herself with needs and desires and a willingness to demand that he answered over and over.

In the carriage house, her hands clenched at her sides. "Why have you come back?" she asked.

"I want you."

She froze as he kissed her.

Her jaw was shut tight. It didn't matter. He

took his time, tasting her lips, a playful bite, a chance to suck and nip and explore. Her cheek was silky, covered with tiny hairs he could skim with his tongue, until he was close enough to inhale the fragrance of her hair, unleashed by heat, like the perfume behind her ear. He kissed that too, listening to her rapid breaths.

"Do I scare you that much?"

Her mouth was dry, her heart thudding against her rib cage, as empty as this room.

"It's not as simple as just wanting," she said.

"Sleep with me again, find out."

"No!" She pushed him away; he barely moved. But she'd broken the spell. "There's a difference between nostalgia and going into heat."

"Is there? Both involve wanting what we don't have. We can have it again, Marcie."

"And you'd be only too glad to oblige." She didn't like the sound of her voice, the raggedness, the desperation.

She ran down the stairs, risking splinters as she gripped the handrail. She slapped a ledger closed and began snapping off lights. "If you think I can be that cavalier about sex with a man who is almost a stranger—"

"You were before."

She punched a button and another light went out. "That was different."

"How?"

"I needed a teacher."

"What do you need now, Marcie?" His soft mocking words carried into the separate office.

"To be cynical and calculating and scratch some itch with you. Is that what you want to hear? I think your offer stinks."

Ray's short curse was as brittle as her voice.

"We either move on or lay this to rest once and for all."

He caught her arm as she reached for her coat. They stood still beside the hall tree in the only pool of light left in the room. Darkness gathered around them like a conspiracy. "Prove me wrong. Show me memory is better than any reality we might have."

A challenge, a taunt. If he only knew how close she was to heeding that urgent voice in the dark.

The outer door was swollen with moisture, it screeched as she opened it. Searching through her bag, she found the key to lock up. "The tour down memory lane is over."

"Why are you running?"

"Because you're cornering me!" She was practically panting, unsure where the rush of emotion came from. "This is all I have now. Don't you see? When I had you—I—I almost gave it all up. And what for?"

"Almost? You told me to take a hike."

Her voice was faint in the whipping wind. "You didn't argue."

"You're a girl who makes up her mind. I didn't think there was any point." But it was beginning to dawn on him there might have been a chance. He would have seen it, if he hadn't been so sure he was wrong for her.

"I was nineteen, Ray." Her voice stopped on a choked sob. She had control of it when she spoke again. "I would have gone with you anywhere, left everything behind. Me, levelheaded, mature, dependable Marcie. If you'd wanted me, you certainly didn't try very hard."

She sighed as if resigned to the truth. She

walked toward the house, not expecting him to follow.

The question he'd dismissed as unimportant haunted him. It was urgent that he know. "I asked you before if you'd ever loved me. You didn't answer."

"I thought it was so obvious. I was crazy about you. Crazy, addicted, ready to throw over my plans, my parents' expectations, all of it. Maybe it was better we did end it. I would have followed you around like some itinerant farmer—"

"I wasn't that poor."

Marcie smiled softly at the sound of wounded pride. "If we *had* married, you wouldn't have been any richer."

"You think that's why I wanted you? For your money?"

Wanted, he said. Not loved. Marcie blinked her eyes and fought tears that wouldn't be stopped. "I'm only saying we might have ended up dragging each other down."

"Bull. With a woman like you I could have—"

"Could have what?" She stopped abruptly, turning on him. This hurt entirely too much. At the moment all she wanted was to get in the house, shut the door, cry her eyes out, and not think why. "Could you have founded a company without me? Made millions? You did that anyway. Please stop hounding me about the past, what I felt, what you did." Not that she knew, and she still couldn't ask, not with the tears wet on her cheeks. "It would be so much easier if you'd just leave. Please go."

He did, knowing she wouldn't appreciate his seeing her in tears. Hating the fact that he was helpless to stop them.

* * *

Monday morning came about six hours too soon. Marcie was groggy and grumpy from spending half the night reexamining her entire life. Only Judge Rosen's previous tart comments to late jurors spurred her to get out of bed.

She arrived at the courthouse at seven-thirty; Ray at seven fifty-five. She recognized the tactic, silently awarding him a point, then immediately subtracting it for unoriginality. He was going to play hard to get. Perhaps he recognized the steely glint in her eyes—on those two occasions he let her catch his eye.

She'd admitted she'd loved him. He hadn't said the same. Bursting into tears was far from her favorite means of dealing with disagreements. In fact, she couldn't remember the last time she'd done it. Age eight, perhaps.

Very well. It was done. That didn't mean they were. They'd gotten more honest talking done the night before than in the last three weeks.

She'd discovered at approximately three-thirty that morning that she was a woman who feared any emotion she couldn't control. If she sent Ray away again, it *would* be easier. She'd never have to worry again, or cry the way she had, or get into incredibly embarrassing emotional messes. Or risk ever being so ecstatically happy. At eighty, looking back on life, she'd be able to say she'd never made a fool of herself over a man. And she'd have her orderly, hollow life to prove it.

Staring out over the lawns from her window, Marcie wanted more than that. After ten years with her life on emotional hold, she had another chance to love, laugh, risk. She wanted that risk.

"It could lead to loving Ray again," she said, her breath stirring the filmy curtains. He might not love her as overwhelmingly as she was capable of loving him. But what was risk if you had all the answers going in? "No more playing it safe."

She was going after the man who'd taught her about love. Now he'd teach her about emotions, that they could be savored, not stunted. *Teach me. Teach me where I went wrong.*

As dawn melted the gray mist on the horizon, she smiled. She almost felt sorry for Ray Crane. The nineteen-year-old had nothing on the grown woman when it came to getting her way.

"Eleven and twelve," the bailiff counted off. "Will the jury file in please?"

Marcie didn't worry. They had one more week to go. She'd catch him in the hallway, by the coat-rack, at a lunch counter. And she'd nail him to the wall.

But first they had the trial to finish.

She paused before mounting the step up into the jury box. Ray almost banged into her. He didn't offer a hand up, the bailiff did. Marcie paused for a fraction of a second longer, then, chin lifted, walked regally to the end and sat down in a very satisfied manner. Grace Kelly couldn't have been cooler. Her hair was loose and brushed back, every strand in place. The suit was Chanel, winter white with gold buttons. The hose were sheer silk; she took her time crossing the legs they encased. She looked at the defendant's table, the prosecutor's table, then up at Ray.

His eyes ricocheted from her legs to her brilliant smile.

"Good morning," she said.

He ground his teeth so tightly, a vein stood out on his jaw.

She touched his leg. He almost hit the ceiling.

Seven

"All right, people," Judge Rosen announced, "for the record, this is a continuation of last week's case, the People versus Walter Steinbeck. I take it you remembered not to discuss the case over the weekend?"

The jury shook their heads. "It was the farthest thing from my mind," Marcie cooed under her breath. As the judge continued with some legal preliminaries, she placed her hand on the arm-rest, fingertips resting oh so lightly on Ray's cuff. He used that hand to loosen, then tighten, his tie. He smoothed the flap. He looked at the clock.

Fidgeting like an overgrown schoolboy at a too-small desk, Marcie thought. Or a man in an electric chair.

Ray swallowed, his tie doing extra duty as a choke collar. You'd think the world was designed for pygmies, not men. The criminals should be made to feel uncomfortable, not the jurors. The damned chair was squeezing him, the courtroom was stuffy, and it was only eight A.M. Perfume assaulted him from both sides, but one scent stood out—Marcie's. He wished it wouldn't. It had been on his clothes when he'd picked them up off the floor that morning, insinuating its way into his closet, his life.

She was being nice to him. Practically flirtatious. Why? He'd gotten the answer he sought, the one about whether she'd ever loved him. She had, and he'd been a fool not to see it. That should have settled it. Maybe she hadn't rejected him as coldly as he'd once thought, but she'd certainly done it the previous night. Firmly. And in tears. How was he to win her back now? A man had his pride.

And the prosecution had a case to try. And Ray had to sit beside Marcie Courville until it was finished. Meanwhile, the defense had done nothing more than cross-examine, casting doubt on every substantial piece of testimony so far. Ray weighed what he'd heard, waiting for that one fact that would declare Steinbeck guilty of more than mismanagement.

"I would like to call Emily Steinbeck," the prosecutor announced.

She had on a mink stole, the kind he'd once seen Marcie's mother wear driving through town. But that was old money. The ex–Mrs. Steinbeck smelled of new money, freshly minted and quickly spent. The rock on her right hand glittered so brightly, one would never guess diamonds came from the ground. Same for the earrings. She wore the stole into the witness box.

Not an eye left her as Spannick proceeded slowly across the carpet. "Mrs. Steinbeck, how long have you been divorced from Walter Steinbeck?"

"Three months," she said with gusto. "We were afraid it wouldn't come through in time."

Obviously, she'd been waiting eagerly for this day. Ray wondered briefly what could ever unite a woman as self-possessed as she and a man as rumpled and downtrodden as Walter Steinbeck. He seemed to be shrinking in his seat even as she spoke.

Spannick's slight frown of disapproval tempered Emily Steinbeck's next answers. "Just answer the questions, please. And during those years, could you tell us how much money your husband *told you* he made?"

Hazelton rose. "Hearsay, Your Honor?"

"Reword, Mr. Spannick."

"Mrs. Steinbeck, did you have any knowledge of your husband's actual earnings?"

"I saw his paycheck. It didn't look like much."

Steinbeck shrunk a little further. Ray told himself to concentrate on the testimony, sympathy had to be set aside.

"And did you know his position? His title?"

"I thought I did," she replied sharply, patting her frosted hair and smoothing out her lipstick, one lip pressed tightly to the other.

By the time she was finished, Mrs. Steinbeck had testified quite convincingly that her husband was a no-account social climber who'd married above his station, then stole money to support a lifestyle he could never have afforded otherwise. She'd also convinced Ray Crane that Walter Steinbeck had never stood a chance around his wife.

Marcie took a slow, deep breath. It didn't look good for the defendant. However, with every other witness the defense attorney had been able to cast just enough doubt. . . .

She tightly folded her hands. Wasn't this the picture she'd painted for Ray? The potential consequences of a woman raised to money marrying a man she was too young to love. A man subtly driven to crime to impress her, to keep that unworthy love? She wished they could talk.

Ray's hazel eyes were steely, his expression fixed as he stared at Mrs. Steinbeck, listening to a litany of how important her family had always been in the community. Sensing Marcie's gaze, he glanced over, but his dark look was unreadable.

"Prosecution is finished with the witness, Your Honor."

Hazelton stood, touching a burgundy handkerchief to his upper lip like a cat who's just dined on a fat, juicy canary and is ready for the next course. He stuffed the silk back in his breast pocket and began gently, as if picking up the thread of a conversation. "You said earlier, if I may quote, 'We were afraid the divorce wouldn't come through in time.' Who was we?"

"Me and my lawyers."

"Why is that?"

"Because I couldn't testify if we were married. That's the law."

"And you wanted very much to testify."

She puffed herself up, the stole balanced on an impressive bosom. "I know the truth."

"Lucky you," Hazelton replied tartly. "You said lawyers. The dissolution of this unhappy marriage required more than one?"

She shifted on the seat, tugging on her fur-lined armor. "I had one lawyer, however others in his office were gracious enough to offer advice from time to time."

"And what office is that?"

The Publisher of Loveswept® Romances invites you to:

CLAIM A FREE EXCLUSIVE ROMANCE

Lift Here

...PLUS SIX ROMANCES RISK FREE

6 ROMANCES FREE

Detach and affix this stamp to the postage-paid reply card and mail at once!

NO OBLIGATION TO BUY!
THE FREE GIFT IS YOURS TO KEEP

SEE DETAILS INSIDE

LET YOURSELF BE LOVESWEPT BY... SIX BRAND NEW LOVESWEPT ROMANCES!

Because Loveswept romances sell themselves ...we want to send you six (Yes, six!) exciting new novels to enjoy for 15 days — risk free! — without obligation to buy

Discover how these compelling stories of contemporary romances tug at your heart strings and keep you turning the pages. Meet true-to-life characters you'll fall in love with as their romances blossom. Experience their challenges and triumphs — their laughter, tears and passion.

Let yourself be Loveswept! Join our **at-home reader service!** Each month we'll send you six new Loveswept novels **before they appear in the bookstores.** Take up to **15 days to preview** current selections **risk-free! Keep only those shipments you want.** Each book is yours for only $2.09 plus postage & handling, and sales tax where applicable — **a savings of 41¢ per book** off the cover price.

NO OBLIGATION TO BUY — WITH THIS RISK-FREE OFFER!

YOU GET SIX
ROMANCES RISK FREE...
Plus AN EXCLUSIVE TITLE FREE!

Loveswept Romances

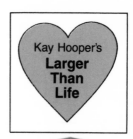

"I don't see what that has to do—"

Hazelton tilted his head, a grim smile on his face. He didn't have to say "answer the question." He let the silence stretch.

Emily Steinbeck huffed. As the star witness she clearly expected better treatment. "Hopkins, Spannick, Goudall, and Kemp. Happy?"

Her voice got very sharp when she was being sarcastic, Marcie noticed. The stole got another tug.

Hazelton slowly reiterated her answer for the jury's sake. "You're saying that your lawyer is a partner in the firm where Mr. Spannick is a partner, that is, until he took a leave of absence to become county prosecutor." His words gained speed and volume, pressing Emily Steinbeck back in her seat as he closed in on her. "Did he help you decide to go through with the divorce? To firm up his case against your husband? A husband you obviously wish to punish for not keeping you in the style you insisted on becoming accustomed to?"

"What am I supposed to answer to all that?" she squawked. But Hazelton barely paused.

"Don't look to Mr. Spannick now, Mrs. Steinbeck. He can't coach you any more!"

"Objection! Your Honor!"

"You're right, Mr. Spannick. Mr. Hazelton, you know about making accusations like that in court. Histrionics is one thing . . ."

"Yes, sir. I withdraw the remark." He didn't withdraw his smirk to the jury. Slowly he circled back to the witness stand, like a shark smelling blood in the water. "Mrs. Steinbeck, did your husband ever tell you he was stealing on your behalf?"

"He said he did it all for me."

"Is that a direct quote?"

"Yes," she hissed. " 'I did it all for you,' he said. The police were pounding on the door at the time."

" 'I did it all for you.' " Hazelton ruminated on that for a moment. "Did what? Work his fingers to the bone and never get more from you than the credit card bill? Put in seventy-hour weeks so you could complain about his never accompanying you to the country club?"

"I won't answer that. That's insulting!"

"That's your testimony, Mrs. Steinbeck. In your deposition you complain about his long hours cutting into your social life. Did anyone besides yourself hear him say 'I did it all for you?' "

"No. But my opinion counts for something."

"We want testimony, not opinions. At your urging, your husband finally 'got up the backbone,' as you put it, to push for what he deserved. Bigger paychecks began coming in."

"Don't you make it sound like I planned any of this. I've been humiliated enough as it is. A criminal for a husband, a failure. I always knew he was worthless."

"Yet you married him."

She flicked open a designer handbag and pulled out a linen handkerchief. She patted her eyes although they appeared dry.

Marcie hadn't seen such obvious playing to the crowd since Hazelton stood up.

"I was foolish and young," Mrs. Steinbeck said, unable to convince anyone that she had ever been either.

"You've testified that he supported you by turning to embezzlement."

"I don't see how else he could have gotten the money."

"So you've testified. And yet, you've kept the minks, the jewels, the house."

Suddenly there was no pretense at tears. She clutched the handkerchief as if it were a live grenade. "These are mine."

"How can they be? They were bought with—"

"Oh no, you don't!" She was halfway out of her seat, the microphone unnecessary as her shrill voice carried across the courtroom. "These are mine, and you can't take them away. I know you can't. I made sure of that with Mr. Spannick when I agreed to testify—"

There was a gasp and all heads turned toward the prosecutor. He did everything in his power to show no reaction. That in itself was a reaction.

"Tell us, Mrs. Steinbeck," Hazelton practically purred, "exactly what sort of deal did you make with Mr. Spannick for your testimony? How much of the money you claim your husband stole were you going to keep?"

Emily Steinbeck sputtered with rage, her eyes ricocheting from Hazelton to Spannick and back. Then she rose majestically, resettled her stole, and hurled here purse directly at Hazelton's head. The courtroom erupted, and the bailiff scurried across to subdue the witness. The judge pounded his gavel.

Ray stole a glance at Marcie. Her eyes were so wide, he had to smile. She smiled back. "Good heavens," she murmured under her breath. He squeezed her hand.

Spannick was on his feet. "Objection! Objection!"

"Sustain, Your Honor, that's fine with me," Hazelton shouted over the hubbub, handing the purse to the bailiff. He waved a hand dismissively at the witness and completed the gesture by smoothing back his hair. "This was purchased testimony. I believe the jury has seen all they need to see."

The judge bristled and pounded his gavel one more time. "They've seen a damn circus. That is the *last* outburst we'll have in this trial. Hazelton, are you done?"

Mr. Hazelton made a little move and tightened the knot in his tie. "With this so-called witness? Yes, Your Honor."

"Then sit! Mr. Spannick, any redirect? No? All right, Mrs. Steinbeck—" The woman was in tears in earnest this time, sobbing on the witness stand. "You may step down. And consider yourself fortunate I don't throw you in jail for that. Who is the next witness for the prosecution?"

Spannick rose slowly, watching his star witness toss him a hateful glare as she shuffled out of the courtroom. He swallowed so hard, Ray could see his Adam's apple bob. "We have none, Your Honor."

"Then we're ready for the defense."

Hazelton stood calmly behind the defense table, one hand on his coat lapel à la Abe Lincoln, the other resting reassuringly on the shoulder of his client. "The defense"—there was a studied pause— "rests."

Ray and Marcie both managed to contain their gasps of surprise. The rest of the jury wasn't so lucky. The judge picked up his gavel for two hard knocks, pink splotches standing out on his cheeks. "Is that all you have to say?" he growled at Hazelton.

"I believe the prosecutor's case has been shown to be as full of holes as—"

"Save the summing up for after lunch." Judge Rosen glared across the courtroom at the clock over the doors. It was only ten forty-five, but there was no way he'd continue with spirits running so high. "Back at one o'clock, and I mean everybody. Concluding arguments and jury instructions will take place; we should start deliberations by three." He turned on the jury with a weak attempt at a smile. "This is where you people get to do what you were picked to do. Dismissed!"

As they rose, Marcie realized her hand was still in Ray's, and had been all the time. It felt so right. But they had other business to contend with first. Reluctantly, she let go.

So that was the case. Marcie pondered the theatrics of it all as she and the other jurors got through a long but subdued lunch. Hazelton had simply thrown in the towel. But he'd also thrown up a lot of dust. A shadow of a doubt had been his entire defense. Would it do the trick?

She kept harking back to Mrs. Steinbeck. The regal bearing, the lofty tones, the haughty air. And the way poor Walter Steinbeck had stared at her like a starving dog eyeing a steak. He'd been a poor boy, no doubt astounded at the wife he'd managed to catch, and equally ignorant of how to keep her.

But had he embezzled the money?

"He didn't take the stand," Mr. Gear, the realtor, mumbled from the other end of the table.

"Shh," someone else said. "We'll have plenty of time to go over it in the jury room."

He grumbled and took a big bite of his hamburger.

A few jurors looked at Marcie. She'd been chosen as their forewoman. In a few hours she'd be organizing this thing.

Thanks, Ray, she thought wryly.

And if it was over so soon? What about her and Ray?

She set down her salad fork and patted her lipstick with a paper napkin. It wasn't over yet.

After a few minutes of uncomfortable quiet in their private room, the jurors were off and running.

"He's innocent."

"Think so?"

"If the owner hadn't died and a new owner come in to learn the ropes—"

"He did give himself quite a raise."

"Yes he did."

"That doesn't look good."

Ray's suggestion cut through the hubbub. "Perhaps we can start by looking at embezzlement charges for the money he actually took, the four-hundred-percent pay increase and bonus."

Everyone paused.

"Guess that's a possibility."

"Does that mean we're letting him off for the whole hundred thou?"

"That only means we narrow our focus and tackle one count at a time."

Marcie took a deep breath to calm the jitters in her stomach, rose from her place at the head of the table, and thanked Ray. Fortunately, her voice had a steady, church garage-sale tone to it that her mother would have heartily approved of. "Ladies and gentlemen. As your elected forewoman, instead of going around and around on the possibilities, which, as we're all aware, Mr. Spannick tried to make as clear-cut as possible and Mr. Hazelton tried to make as murky as possible, I concur with Mr. Crane that we get to work on count one, the unauthorized raise."

"Allegedly unauthorized," Mr. Gear said.

Marcie raised an eyebrow. She hadn't expected a not guilty tilt from Gear. He caught her meaning.

"Just playing devil's advocate," he added.

Great, she thought. With what appeared to be an evenly divided jury, the last thing she needed was someone leaning one way and voting the other. "Thank you, Mr. Gear."

She crossed to the chalkboard that had been wheeled in. Every eye was on her. She felt responsible, alone. Ray would make a wonderful ally at a time like this, if they'd been on speaking terms. As it was, the other jurors perceived them as a couple anyway. Knowing that it wasn't true hurt more than it should.

The chalk made a crisp grating sound as she drew a white line down the board. "On the left I'm going to put the six points the judge gave us which have to be proved to convict. On the right I'll make two more columns, one pro, one con."

"He's going to be a con."

"We'll get to that," she replied frostily over her shoulder. She felt like a schoolmarm, but she also sensed their relief that someone was taking charge, otherwise they'd have argued all night.

"The first count is the unauthorized pay raise and bonus Steinbeck supposedly got for setting up these corporations."

"The nerve of the guy, paying himself for all the work he put into embezzling, and his boss dying in the hospital."

"He didn't look that nervy."

"Not at all."

"Almost a caricature of a mild-mannered accountant, if you ask me."

"Maybe caricature is the important word here," Ray put in. "It might be an act his lawyer drummed up."

"If we could get back to the point," Marcie interrupted. She also sensed Ray leaning toward conviction. The thought had her pulse thrumming a bit harder, since she wasn't exactly convinced. The last thing they needed was a showdown over this.

"Looks are not testimony," she said somewhat portentously. "I noticed some of you fidgeting during the trial, that doesn't mean *you're* guilty."

Appreciative chuckles and a long look from Ray. Now he knew she'd been watching him out of the corner of her eye all week, as intensely aware of him as he'd been of her.

Marcie whirled back to the board. "The charge for embezzlement is as follows. . . ."

Eight

Voices erupted all around the table. They'd been at it for several hours. Marcie, trying to pick up the major points, suddenly wished she had a gavel of her own. Ray glanced darkly into his coffee, scanned the table for a few moments, and slapped his palm down. Stunned silence followed, heads turned from Ray to Marcie and back again.

"One at a time, the lady's getting rattled," he growled.

Marcie took comments from all of the jurors. "Then we're divided on count five."

" 'Fraid so," someone said.

"Let's go on to count six: Defendant must have intended to defraud or cheat his employer."

It was the same issue all over again. "How do we know what he intended?" one juror asked.

Marcie found the answer in her pile of papers. "The judge gave us the instructions for the legal definition of specific intent. I'll pass them around."

While they were being read, Marcie recalled the reasonable doubt instructions. One phrase in particular stood out, Judge Rosen's voice sounding in her head. "Reasonable doubt is a state of mind which would cause you to hesitate in making an important decision in your personal life."

Exactly. Her personal life was sitting at the other end of the table. And this might be the last day they'd be on jury duty together.

Ray looked up, his eyes boring into her, bringing heat to her cheeks and a delicious shivery feeling to her abdomen. He wiped a drop of coffee off the corner of his mouth with a thumb. She remembered the way he'd run that thumb over her lips. It seemed a hundred years ago. She wasn't going back into that cocoon of responsibility, of duty. She was going to risk loving him, if he'd let her.

He went back to his coffee as all heads bent over the papers. All along he'd seemed coldly critical of Steinbeck. She dreaded the first vote.

"Okay, so specific intent means he had to have done this knowing it was wrong. Did he?"

"He tried to bribe the auditor."

"Yes."

"That man's testimony didn't end with *him* throwing a purse."

"So Steinbeck seems to have intended to hide the shell corporations he created."

"Secreted," Gear repeated with relish.

"He begged the auditor not to reveal it. We've got testimony on that."

"For the other side?" Marcie had the feeling she was conducting the trial all over again.

"The poor man was working sixty-hour weeks, on average, and the auditor was interfering with his work."

"So the auditor says."

"But Steinbeck wouldn't let the diskette out of his sight. Even took it home with him at night."

"His secretary testified to that."

"Kind of suspicious, don't you think?"

"Well." Marcie made her last check mark, looking over the already crowded chalkboard. She decided to take the bull by the horns. If she and Ray were divided on this, it was time to face it. "Shall we argue over whether the owner consented to Steinbeck's creating these corporations and paying himself from them, or should we take a first ballot just to see where we stand?"

The jurors voted to vote. The tally was six for conviction, six against. Marcie smiled a brave smile, hoping to reassure the antsiest among them that this would be resolved one way or the other. Unconsciously, she tugged up her sleeves. "Looks like we're going to have a little more discussion."

Four hours later, tensions were running higher. The deli sandwiches were gone. Plastic wrap and empty mustard packets littered the table, along with soda pop cans and empty cups.

"Marcie? We haven't heard your opinion."

Marcie's heart thumped at the sound of Ray's voice. She was practically tearing her hair out to keep this orderly, but her own emotions were a jumble every time he looked her way. "I'd have to say he's innocent unless proven guilty."

"So is every man," he challenged quietly.

She wished she could stare into his eyes long enough to know exactly what he meant. Unfortunately, it wasn't the time or place to talk about it. Drawing herself up in her chair, without conscious thought she adopted the rounded tones and careful word choice her mother would have used. "The prosecution hasn't proven that Mr. Eldredge *didn't* give verbal authorization."

"That he ever did is only Hazelton's contention," Ray reminded her. "Steinbeck didn't testify to that fact."

"I know, I know." She rubbed her forehead. "But Spannick hasn't proven it didn't happen, and according to these instructions he has to. The burden is on him."

Gear grunted in disgust. "The burden is on us, if you ask me."

There were audible sighs, and a long silence settled over the jury.

"I gotta make a trip to the can."

Marcie pursed her lips. "Perhaps Mr. Gear has a point here. Let's see if the bailiff will let us take another break."

Marcie and Ray met by the coffeepot again.

"Holding up?" he asked quietly.

"After four cups of coffee in four hours, my throat is dry and my nerves are jangling."

"It's not very good."

"Even Sandy's Turkish Delight would taste good right now."

He moved down the table to the artificial creamer and packets of sugar.

"Ray."

Her voice stopped him. She touched his arm anyway. "We can discuss this now," she said softly. "That's what we're here for."

He didn't answer immediately, tearing open a packet of sugar, watching the granules disappear into the swirling cream.

"You don't seem very sympathetic to Mr. Steinbeck," Marcie stated.

"With a wife like that?"

"That's what I mean."

He hadn't overlooked the similarities of this case to theirs. "If the poor slob didn't know better than to wallow like a kicked dog for that woman, I have no sympathy for him whatsoever. A man should know who he is and where he stands."

"But if there's even a shadow of a doubt that someone is guilty, you have to let them off," she said. "You have to forgive, no matter what mistakes someone might have made in the past."

His mouth crooked, but it wasn't much of a smile. "Forgiveness is for people who do wrong. What did you and I ever do wrong except fall in love?"

Marcie's heart lurched. Had he loved her? For so long she'd categorized their affair as a humiliating one, a lovesick girl acting on an infatuation. Perhaps her emotions hadn't been so off base. "Maybe falling in love was the only right thing we did. I was wrong to drive you away."

"Think so?"

"I want to try again, Ray."

The room could have dissolved around them, the planet could have stopped. The only movement was the lowering of his gaze from her hair to her eyes to her mouth.

"Maybe we'd better sit down again." He took his seat.

At ten o'clock that night the judge let them go home. Tomorrow they'd be back for a full day of deliberations. To Marcie, operating on three hours sleep, it was almost too exhausting to think about. She combed back her hair, studying herself in her bedroom mirror.

She'd laid it on the line today. "I want to try again." He hadn't exactly jumped at the prospect.

Well, what did she expect? He wasn't going to fall at her feet in the jury room!

But he should call, a softer voice said.

Oh no. Just because I think I might love him doesn't mean I'm going to become one of those women who sits by the phone. It's almost eleven. We were busy all day, we'll be busy tomorrow—

The doorbell chimed. A tremor like a low musical note vibrated through her. Her hand shook slightly as she set down her brush and went downstairs.

"Ray." Her heart did somersaults, her mouth went dry. "Come in."

"Do you mind?"

"Not at all."

"We've had a long day."

"I was just thinking that. But it would be a longer night if we didn't settle this."

Settle it. Did that mean end it? she wondered. Ray stepped over the threshold and looked up two stories of curving staircase.

"You never saw the house, did you?"

"You never invited me in."

"You would have turned me down," she chided softly.

"True. I probably would have."

They stood listening to the silence of the house. Although the intervening walls divided it into condominiums, it was still massive.

"How about a fresh start?" she suggested suddenly. "You, me, my humble abode."

"Humble?" He gave a brief laugh and let her lead the way. His emotions were tangled enough without her making fun of him.

He had this uncomfortable feeling that his blind spot where Marcie was concerned was becoming more like a lunar eclipse. The previous night, in tears, she'd asked him to stop hounding her. That day she'd flirted with him in the jury box, as pleasant as you please and beautiful as ever, if you discounted the faint circles under her eyes. She'd come right out and said she wanted them to try again. And he, like a stray dog, couldn't stay away. As they toured the house one emotion came to the fore, familiar as a sore tooth: He felt thoroughly outclassed.

Grass wallpapers, cherry desks, handwoven carpets. For a house divided by six, the conversion had been tastefully done. And yet Marcie was calmly, competently dismantling her home. He wondered aloud what that meant to her.

"I certainly couldn't keep it up myself. I'd spend too much time thinking of the way it used to be."

As was he. He watched her move, the unconscious grace, the slope of her shoulders. In jeans she had a tidy rear end. She looked immaculate, chic, sexy, all at once. When they reached the top of the stairs he towered over her. But there was no cowering in her, there never had been. As a woman she stood up to him, the determined Marcie, the Marcie who's set her mind on something. She made his heart pump overtime.

They were in the upstairs reading room, where hand-carved raised paneling glowed with polish. The wallpapers here were vine patterned, the couches of heavily flowered chintz. Round end tables were draped with fabric and cluttered with silver picture frames. The room spoke of old money.

Ray breathed a silent sigh of relief when they entered a freshly painted kitchenette, bleached wood floors separating it from the older rooms. He sniffed the tart resiny smell of construction. Crane Corporation might do offices instead of homes, but Ray knew quality when he saw it.

When he asked, she told him the name of the company involved, what the schedules and over-runs had been.

"Too bad."

"Did I pay too much?"

"No." He grinned. "I was thinking if you had, I could have ridden to your rescue, scattering contractors in my wake. Doesn't look like you needed my services at all."

She shared his laughter, said something appropriate. That was kind of her, he thought, unaccountably disgruntled. "What's up there?"

"The third floor. My room, mostly." Blue eyes flitted, looked away.

"I always was curious about your bedroom."

"I'm sure you were." She gave a short, breathy laugh. "How about if I get us some coffee?"

"Sure." Ray hesitated before stepping onto the pearl-pink carpeting. He checked his shoes, scowled, and took the last flight of stairs to her room.

"So what's your professional opinion?" If she was surprised to find him standing at her vanity, she hid it well.

She set a tray on the foot of the bed, coffee and a handful of cookies on an oval china plate made just for that purpose. She was calm and collected. Not him.

Ray glanced out the French doors overlooking the small wrought-iron balcony. The canopy over the bed caught his eye once more. "Why didn't you put on a strand of pearls?"

"Pardon?"

"You're playing the perfect hostess."

"Uh-oh. Score one for you. Too bad I don't have my chalkboard handy." She sat carefully on the bed, not wanting to jostle the tray.

Ray felt the same way about the balance of his teetering emotions. Unaccustomed caution met the drumbeat urge of emotion caused by seeing Marcie on a bed, any bed.

Light, softly cast by a bedside lamp, shimmered over her. The shade matched the drapes, the wallpaper, both as pink as her cheeks.

She plucked at the bedspread. Marcie flustered, imagine that. Ray's mouth slanted in a smile. He could afford that much. Leaning against the French door, he crossed one long leg over the other. "I wanted to see where you sleep, the balcony you used to signal me from."

"I thought we weren't here for memories."

That left open the question of what he was there for. Suddenly the air was brittle and dry. He twisted the doorknob shaped like an iron *S*. Air whistled in, curtains fluttered like pulses.

Marcie knew she should stand. The bed was no place—no, the bed was the perfect place, but not for the kind of discussion she wanted to have. "We can talk about this."

"I'd rather do something about it."

"Like what?" she asked, tipping her chin up, daring herself, him.

"Like this."

The kiss was deliberate, tantalizing. He took it

very easy. She didn't fight. She wanted it as much as he ever had. He still did.

Reaching between them for a suit-coat button, his hand brushed the bottom edge of her breast. He cupped her and she trembled, swelling, filling his hand. She exhaled raggedly when his hands lifted to explore her hair, fine-spun threads running through his fingers.

"You keep wanting to show me what's changed," he urged, "show me what hasn't. Us. The one thing we know we have."

He was undoing the gold buttons of her cardigan, spreading it as he wiped the silk of her blouse from waist to breast.

"I used to dream you'd come back," she whispered. "I could never tell you how much."

"Tell me now."

But the words were stolen by sensations when he raked her neck with his tongue, his teeth tracing her collarbone, tugging a strap off her shoulder.

Her hands were on him now, shaking, fumbling, not knowing where to begin. She could only hold on, dizzy and weak. "Oh!"

The doors to the balcony blew open, cold night air filled the room. She moved to close them, one hand on each door.

He came up behind her, letting her feel him there at her back as he spread his arms along hers, reached around to open her blouse.

"Someone might see."

His dark voice was beside her ear. "I don't care." The last button undone, he opened her to the night. "Do you?"

"No." She shook her head, hair sweeping her shoulders like a shower of gold, slippery against his chest. She turned in his arms, pressing a kiss to his chest for every button she flicked open—until she reached the fifth and felt the muscles of his abdomen ripple. "I used to dream of us in this room. You'd come back—"

"We're not dreaming." His voice grated, his mouth set.

"—I'd find you in the garden, on the grass. Oh please, Ray. I want it again. Everything we can be together."

He swept her up in his arms, set her down on the bed. "This is no dream."

Not with the clinking of a tray being set on the floor. Not with rasp of his zipper, the *thunk* of two shoes on thick carpet. Not with the lights on and the air making her shiver. She covered herself.

He stood at the end of the bed between the wispy curtains. Clutching the quilt, he gave it a jerk, stripping it off in one motion. "If you're cold, tell me."

"Will you close the doors?"

He shook his head, then took off the last of his clothes. "I'll make you hot."

Nine

She rolled under him. "Please," she whispered.

Everything felt disjointed, heightened, a searing flash of memory awash in a tide of reality.

He teased and withdrew with his hands, his tongue. One massive hand was on her back, his fingers curled in the waistband of her jeans, inching inside.

Her hands were cold when she reached between them, he flinched at her touch. Her laugh was throaty, liquid.

"You sure you want me to?" She chuckled, the sound rumbling in her throat.

He growled, it was the only sane response he could make. She took it as an affirmative.

He yowled and jumped back. "Damn they're cold!"

"I told you so." She smiled, with a sleepy, heavy-lidded look. "They'll get warmer."

"There won't be anything left for them to touch."

"Feels all right to me." Her eyes fluttered open, and she looked up at him, her hands indeed getting warmer, catching his heat, creating warmth through friction.

"Marcie, you're going to make me explode."

"I want to take you someplace you've never been."

"I've been here before."

"Not crazy, not like you made me. I want to drive *you* over the edge."

"You always did. Don't you remember?"

"I was too wiped out by what you did to me."

"With you." His tender emphasis tore at her heart.

She mewed. He remembered. She stroked, he felt it in his shuddering bones. Her hair was spread on the quilt like an angel's halo, but her touch was wanton. If she didn't know what she was doing to him, she was about to learn the most thorough lesson he'd ever given her.

"Marcie," he warned when her grip tightened.

"When we were younger, I was ready for the lovemaking, not the emotions. Show me how. I want you to teach me again."

"Again?"

"Please."

He tensed, the air suddenly clammy on his back. "Is that what this is, more lessons?"

She rubbed a palm over his shoulders, mistaking the tension for another kind. "I remember some of what you taught me." Her hands found better access, one curling around him in a velvety grip. "Like this."

So that's what it was, Ray thought, his mouth tasting like iron. A relationship on her terms, a paid instructor come to the house to give lessons. And this was how he was paid. He grasped her wrist. "A retainer for my services?"

"Ray!"

He disengaged her grip and sat up. "This is the thanks I get?"

She looked stricken. He was up, dressing, his back to her. She pulled her blouse closed anyway, wishing they had turned out the lights. "You know I didn't mean that. We had, have more than that."

"Lord knows we should. It seems like every time I'm on Courville property, I'm treated like another hired hand."

"Property!" She sputtered at the scathing way he said it, then she lashed out. "If I've ever treated you that way, I said I was sorry."

"For what?" he shouted, the words echoing through the house. "For the fact that you knew I never belonged in your house, in your precious bed? For the fact that you had the good sense to get rid of me when it got too hot?"

"You're twisting my words, making both of us sound cheap!"

"It was free as I recall." And this was getting uglier by the minute.

"Then stop recalling!" Good Lord, now she was screaming at him. She held her head in her hands, listening to him shove in the last of his shirttail and buckle his belt. "Look at me as I am now. Stop blaming me—"

He took her chin roughly in his hand and forced her to look at him. "Baby, the woman I see doesn't want to make a mistake like me again." The carpet muffled his steps as he walked out.

"Where are you going?" She wiped her hair off her face, dismayed to find it in such disarray. She followed him to the top of the stairs, squaring her shoulders. She was not chasing him, a few tattered shreds of pride still clung. "Do you think I planned this? Some sort of reparations for the past?"

"No." He marched down the winding staircase; he was almost to the first floor. "If it was planned, we'd have had little sandwiches with the crusts cut off."

"Oh!"

She stopped thinking, stopped hurting. The red rush of anger coursed through her so fast, she was reaching for the vase before she knew where she'd aim it. She hurtled it downward through the opening until it smashed on the flagstones two stories below. Ray looked up slowly, a startled grin on his face.

Marcie clutched the banister with one hand, the other covering her gaping mouth. "I—I— Are you all right?"

"Never came near me," he replied calmly.

Her anger dashed with the vase, Marcie had trouble working up another head of steam. "Well, I, uh, how dare you say something like that to me."

"Well, I, uh, guess I take it back," he drawled. Walking out into the foyer, he toed the broken shards of porcelain.

"Let me get a broom." Marcie's voice was as fluttery and faraway as her shocked expression.

By the time she got there, Ray was crouching in the center of the main hall, absently turning over a half-dozen shiny glazed pieces. They weren't nearly as glazed as the look in Marcie's eyes. She crouched at the outer edge and immediately started sweeping up with a small whisk broom.

"Very efficient," Ray said. "A man'd think you broke things every day."

She glared furiously at the onyx flagstones, working her way inward. "That it should come to this. Throwing things!"

"I told you, you had a temper."

"You could have been hit!"

"Were you aiming at me?" he asked quietly. His knee bumped her backside. She moved toward the left.

"You know good and well I wasn't."

"Thank goodness for that."

"You could have been hit by a flying piece of— Don't! Don't sit there, you could cut yourself. I haven't swept there yet."

He stood, swiping at his pant leg. "Not everything can be so neatly swept up. Or glued back together." He leaned over her and dropped a jagged piece into the dustpan.

Marcie knew she was close to tears, but there wasn't much she could do about it. Had she ruined everything with this display of ridiculous fury? "Sometimes I think you bring out the absolute worst in me, Ray Crane." Eyes brimming, she looked up at him.

The man had the audacity to grin. "That's what I'm here for."

Humiliation, anger, grief, and for some damn reason gratitude, warred within her. She returned to her sweeping with a vengeance. "You were leaving a moment ago. As I recall, I'd done something unforgivable." Although for the life of her, she couldn't remember what. "Before I threw my tantrum, that is."

"I kind of liked that part."

"Ha. I bet you did." She wiped her running nose on her sleeve, froze, then sighed. "Do you have any idea how old that vase was? How valuable?"

"No," he said shortly.

"Neither do I," she replied after a moment, wide eyed with wonder. She laughed, then laughed some more. Before she knew it, she was sitting on the floor, tears of laughter rolling down her face.

Ray put his hands deep in his pockets and laughed with her.

She loved him all over again. Who else could she blow up at like that? Who else could possibly provoke her? She crossed her legs Indian style and set the dustpan and whisk broom aside. The storm had passed. "I honestly don't know what happens to me when I'm around you."

He shrugged.

"How do I convince you our differences don't matter? If that's really the problem, how do we solve it?"

He pursed his lips, studying the stone inlay, the tip of a scuffed shoe. "Come to the cottage with me."

The idea had just occurred to him—his family's cottage, a log cabin on a reedy little lake well off the beaten path, as far north in Michigan as a person could get without crossing the bridge into the Upper Peninsula. Rustic, unwinterized, it was the only kind of summer home Ray's family could afford.

But they'd be alone, and, for what it was worth, off Courville property.

She sat up straighter and considered his suggestion. Only Marcie could look elegant sitting on a bare floor, wearing nothing but jeans, a hastily donned sweater, and a half-unbuttoned blouse. Ray made it a point to look into her eyes, avoiding the flush between her breasts, the scrap of lacy lingerie. It was harder not to see the flush on her cheeks, the sparkle in her eye.

Emotions were still running high. Her soft "When?" almost had him crossing the floor to her.

"When the trial's over."

"But, the business—"

"Your partner thinks she's going to be managing the shop all week. My own office is running without me. It's Easter weekend, so we'd have three days."

"If we reach a verdict tomorrow." Her heart tumbled. They might not reach a verdict at all— and she was one of the reasons why.

"Maybe we should get some sleep," he said, hand on the doorknob.

She nodded, although she could almost taste the words *Please stay* on her tongue.

"This weekend then." The door closed behind him, a draft of cold air reminded her, her blouse was open.

An unrelated shiver coursed through her. A weekend together. She stood unsteadily, her knee creaking. Pieces of glass tinkled in the dustpan. "Just clear out the breakables before I get there, Mr. Crane." Heavens, what that man did to her!

Marcie tried to keep the sigh out of her voice. Evie Carter, who's said as little as possible the day before, had discovered overnight a real talent for argument. Marcie wondered who she'd gone over all this with and decided it'd be better not to ask. A mistrial at this point would be almost as maddening as the whole jury process.

"May I have a show of hands once more?"

They'd decided cutting those wretched little slips of paper was too time consuming. As she counted the latest results, Marcie would have gladly torn up a hundred strips of paper using her teeth! Mrs. Dozier was now voting *for* conviction, and Melanie Zylowski had switched to acquittal.

Ray's low chuckle was the only thing that kept Marcie from screaming. The look he sent her way reminded her how close they were to the private weekend at the cottage. She and Melanie were the only ones standing in the way of a conviction. She prayed Ray wouldn't be the one to point it out.

Mr. Gear did.

She rescinded the prayer.

"You gotta see, the guy secreted those funds. Told no one. Flashed money all around, acting like a big shot."

"That may be a crime against good taste, but it's not against the law. He never boasted of having embezzled it."

"I've been going over the psychology in my head," Mrs. Dozier said.

"Good place for it," Ray commented wryly.

Mrs. Dozier gave him a tight little smile that crinkled her makeup as she launched into her theory. "Imagine, if you will,"—she ignored the barely stifled moans around the table—"that this is a poor young man in love with a woman who's very concerned with her family and position."

"And?" Marcie asked as politely as possible, easily conjuring up the picture Mrs. Dozier painted.

"Well, they marry. But she never lets him forget who he is and finally, he snaps." She broke a coffee stirrer in half, by way of demonstration. "He's worn down by the burden of her expectations."

Hazelton himself couldn't have been more effective, Marcie thought. Why was it a captive audience brought out the loquaciousness in some people?

"Perhaps you feel sorry for him," Ray said, half question, half statement. Their gazes locked. For once, Marcie couldn't look away.

"Don't *you*?" The question was for them alone.

"I don't envy him his wife."

"Is she the villain in all this?" A pin could have dropped. Marcie knew there was pain in her eyes, but even a gavel shot couldn't have made her blink now. "Are you blaming her for this?" Was that the problem?

Ray pushed the pieces of the broken coffee stirrer together. Like the *I Ching*, maybe the sticks would point the way. "He's thrown his life away trying to live up to someone else's standards." Another piercing look. "I can understand what might drive a man to that. But he also committed a crime, and circumstances don't let him off the hook."

Him, not them. Marcie rubbed her red-rimmed eyes. Was she the one letting their private lives interfere with her decision? Letting the past color the present?

"Miss Zylowski," she said firmly.

"Melanie, please."

"Melanie, I'm not the only holdout here."

"Well," the young woman hedged, "if you want to change your vote, I guess I could change mine."

"That's not how it's done. If you choose to believe he's not guilty, you won't be browbeaten,

I can promise you that. This is a matter of conscience." In Marcie's case, a guilty one.

While Melanie squirmed, the thought reverberated in Marcie's mind. Steinbeck wasn't Ray, no matter how many similarities there might have been. Ray was successful, and he'd come by that the honest way, through hard work. Guilt about the way she'd once treated him could no longer color her sympathy for Steinbeck. Without the emotion, the answer seemed clear.

"I guess he does seem pretty guilty," Melanie conceded.

"Melanie." Marcie fixed her with a stern look. "Have you been swayed by the testimony itself and the discussion that's taken place? Oh dear Lord, now I'm talking like Judge Rosen," she wailed to indulgent smiles. "That is the only basis under which you should change your verdict."

"I guess so."

Ten pairs of eyes fastened on Marcie, waiting for her decision. "May I see another vote then? For guilty on count one?"

Twelve hands went up, Marcie's included.

"Count two?"

The same.

"Counts three through six, the shell corporations?"

The same.

Sighs all around and scattered applause. "Mrs. Wiltse, would you tell the bailiff we've reached a decision?"

They left for the cottage on Thursday, after Marcie had taken an extra day to clear things up at work. And to work up her courage.

The morning was gray and unpromising. She hadn't stopped talking since they'd gotten in the car.

She stammered to a stop. "Don't you think so?"

"I think," Ray said, never taking his eyes from the road, "that for someone who spent almost two full days arguing with a jury, you haven't run down yet."

"Well excuse me."

He laughed at her frosty attitude. The sound of that rumbling voice thawed her a bit.

"I was trying to point out that announcing to a courtroom that you'd found a man guilty of a major felony isn't easy."

"I was there."

Marcie was dying to ask but she couldn't find the words.

"No, your voice didn't shake," he said.

The air left her lungs in a little puff as she laughed. How did he know these things?

"But your hands were." He smiled in the direction of the yellow line. Piles of dirty snow edged the otherwise dry roads heading north. "The paper positively rattled."

"Now you're teasing me."

"Something I plan to do a lot more of."

A shiver darted through her. "At least we didn't have to recommend a sentence."

"Not in this state."

A companionable silence stretched. Marcie crossed her legs and uncrossed them. She shouldn't have thrown her jeans in the wash last night. They'd shrunk, clinging to her in all the wrong places.

"Nervous?" he asked.

"Of course not." Why didn't he take his eyes off

the road? she wondered irritably. It made her feel as if he didn't have to. As if her every move was being communicated to him through vibes, telepathy, electricity.

"We could pretend," he said, as if after much thought.

"That this is just another weekend?" she chimed in. "That we've done it before?"

He shook his head firmly. "Let's say I'm a dashing, tall, handsome man—"

"That'll take some pretending," she replied saucily.

"Watch it. And you've just met me."

"Hmmm. So we have no past?" He nodded as she entertained the idea. It would be an improvement over this self-imposed tension. "But Mother said never go with strangers."

"Tell her I promised you candy." He looked at her this time, a smoldering look in his eyes. The wolfish grin made her wonder exactly what kind of candy he had in mind.

"Why, Mr. Wolf, you practically have fangs."

"The better to eat you—aw hell," he threw his head back and laughed out loud. "You finish it."

She didn't dare finish the thought. However, playacting had to be preferable to all those little flames tingling under her nerve ends, the bottomless-pit sensation in her stomach, the abyss she was on the edge of falling into. "Hard rock candy?" she croaked out.

He fought a grin and lost. "Hard as a rock is right."

"Ray Crane, you have a downright smutty mind."

"You're keeping up with me."

"And you're going ten miles over the speed limit."

"It'll get us there faster." He eased off on the accelerator, not on her. Reaching for her hand, he lifted it to his lips, then placed it on his thigh. "Blame it on my sweet tooth." Again the sideways look; he'd caught her hesitation. "Where did you think I was going to put your hand?"

"I'm sure I don't know."

"I'm not always that crude."

"Only when you need to be."

"It can be effective. You used to like it."

She looked out the windshield, face front, trying to divorce her mind from the way he was pressing her hand to his thigh, insinuating his thumb into her oversensitive palm. Sensations rocketed up and down her arm, a fullness started in her breasts, reverberating from her heart outward.

"I thought we weren't getting into *used to be*s. We're starting fresh."

"You're right. A man and a woman taking a weekend to get to know each other."

And to prove something, Marcie silently amended. She'd show him she loved him for more than his tutoring. And show herself she could love him without being consumed.

When she looked at him again, her hand was palm up, fingers twined with his. Her problem in a nutshell, she thought wryly: Around Ray Crane her body had a mind of its own.

Ten

The driveway was rutted, winding, and darkened by tall pines. It quickly dwindled to two tire tracks and a grass hump curving its way deeper into the forest. Snow lay in patches beside mossy, downed tree trunks. A thin sheath of ice crackled as they drove over puddles. Bare branches scraped the side of the car. They made a final turn and pulled up to a small cabin.

It looked larger than she'd remembered. One and a half stories with a sloping roof. She remembered the bare-bones loft and the screech of the creaky wood-stove doors. The windows were as small as ever, covered with print curtains.

Ray switched off the local country music station. His gaze followed the slant of her legs. She felt a flutter somewhere below her belt line.

"Want to go see the lake?"

He'd been looking at the condition of her boots, not her legs. She kept her voice level although her heart dropped. "Sure."

Ray came around and opened her door. "I like

to go down there first, convince myself I'm really here."

"Make sure the lake is still there?"

"You never know when someone might pull the plug."

They chuckled and walked slowly over the rise, slipping into the routine as if they did this every weekend. Patches of snow were etched with reddish-brown pine needles, as was the muddy path. The lake was oval, reedy. Broken cattails poked through collars of milky ice. Veins of clearer black and a layer of floating water testified to the warming weather.

"Doesn't look very safe," Marcie murmured.

"I wouldn't walk out on it."

"Don't worry," she said jovially. "I didn't plan on leaving the cabin."

His eyes lingered on hers. "No?"

She shivered. You'd think she'd said she never planned to leave the bed. She crossed her arms and covered another shiver. "Maybe we should unpack."

"Let's."

That one word echoed all the way back up the path. Marcie felt his gaze on her back as they walked single file. Drat those tight jeans.

She could tell herself they'd come to talk. "Right, and I'm Rebecca of Sunnybrook Farm," she muttered to herself.

"Pardon?"

"Nothing."

He'd stepped off the path onto the crunching gravel of the drive. Marcie examined the back of the cabin where a few outbuildings stood. There was a snowmobile and an outboard motor sitting on a slab of plywood, spare parts cast into cardboard boxes. Her eye rested on a smaller outbuilding.

Ray caught her look and grinned. "It's a wood-shed. I had indoor plumbing put in five years ago." He tilted his head toward the newer addition. "The whole thing's been added onto on the far side. Uncle Ted's boys use it during deer season. The other cousins come up now and then."

"And you?"

"I put the money into it," he said simply. "It's mostly Dad's and mine."

"It could be all yours, you've done so well."

"Yeah, well." Characteristically, he ducked the compliment. "Dad wants to hang onto his piece of it."

"How is your Dad?"

"Good. Retired. Doing boat motors and small engine repair on the side. He was always tinkering with something. Might stop up this weekend. We usually open the place on Easter weekend."

Family traditions. Something they hadn't shared before.

"Hand me a bag of those groceries," she said, wanting to help.

"No can do."

"Why not?"

"Aw, Marcie, you know I hate to see a lady lifting."

"Aw, shucks, mister, you can forget that right now." She leaned into the car to pick up her suitcase just as he reached for it from the other side. Their hands met on the handle.

"Compromise," he said, his voice strangely hoarse in the confined space.

"I'll carry mine, you carry yours?"

"I'll carry, you unpack."

"Ray."

"Marcie."

"I don't want to fight."

"I was kind of hoping we could wrestle a bit later on."

She ignored the leer. "Let me have it."

"Let me before my back stiffens up and I'm stuck in this position all weekend."

She laughed. He cheated, using the opportunity to tug the bag out of her grip the moment she loosened it.

"That would be, ah, an unusual position to be in," she taunted, prancing up the walk beside him.

"I'm sure we'd figure out a way to manage."

"Mmm, but I could run away every time you tried anything."

"If you've come here for a chaste weekend, you got the wrong guy."

"Just a thought." She opened the door for him with a sweeping bow. "Age before beauty."

He went through, mumbling something about *libbers*. "You try to sneak out of my bed, Miss Courville, you may find a few mousetraps between you and the door."

"Mice? You've got mice here?"

He chuckled. Entering the bedroom, he tossed the suitcase on the bed. "Does a bear—? Never mind."

"Does a bear what?" she asked, pausing in the living room.

"Not an expression you'd be familiar with."

Standing in the cabin, Marcie knew how Ray had felt above the carriage house. The musty, closed-up smell brought back memories. Low ceilings, rag rugs, furniture made up of family castoffs, well worn before they ever got there. Curtains and lampshades with matching prints of ducks and hunting dogs. There was the same black wood stove. With a screen attached so they could watch the fire, lay in front of it.

She walked to the bedroom door and stopped. The bed was a big, dark, walnut affair, with a set of homemade steps to get up into it. Ray stripped off his leather bomber jacket and looked over at her, waiting for her to cross the threshold. Memory was a sense too, and it was going off all over her body.

She opened her mouth. Nothing came out. She had a hundred things to say, to get out of the way before she could cross the line from being lovers to saying "I love you."

"Nervous?" he asked.

"No reason to be."

"That's not an answer."

"Remember when you said sense of smell brings things back?"

"Trying to get me off the scent?" He grinned, but his eyes were steady and cautious. Did she really want him? Did she have any idea how much he wanted her? Maybe that was what was scaring her. It sure as hell had him shaking.

Jokes, Marcie thought vaguely. The man was making puns. At least his mind was still working. Hers was careening like the fly bumping against the windowpane, dizzy and drunk with spring. "Where do you think he came from?"

"It's the first time he's flown in a while." Ray didn't move as she crossed the room to the windowsill. He let her stand there, his voice low, gruff, softly insinuating. "How long has it been since someone took you flying, Marcie?"

She looked at him. Damn him for being gentle. If only he'd take her in his arms, start something, let her stop thinking and just feel.

He touched her face, tracing a cheekbone, her hairline, an earlobe. "We've got the weekend, we won't rush."

He turned to unpack his shaving kit on the dresser, wiped the surface down with a tissue, sending glittering motes of dust dancing in the afternoon light. She glimpsed a pack of condoms.

The fly buzzed.

She heard the alarm clock she'd brought ticking in her suitcase.

"Am I going to need these?" he asked, watching her in the mirror.

"No" would mean she'd come prepared. She hadn't. She nodded.

He set the suitcase on the floor and tugged off a quilt. The mattress was bare. "Only real bed we ever shared."

Her throat was dry. He was unbuttoning his shirt. "Ray."

He grinned. "One weekend. How bad can it be?"

"I—uh . . ."

"Look, we can get this out of the way, or it'll haunt us all weekend."

Her carefully neutral expression crumbled. "That's really romantic!"

He grinned. "You going to get huffy and walk out on me? It's a long way back."

"Oh, so I'm a prisoner now!" She stopped in midtirade and crossed her arms, slanting him a look only when she heard his low chuckle. "And what's so funny about your taking all the romance out of this?"

"How about the way you disguise your fears as self-righteousness? That's good for laugh."

"Fears? Of what?"

"What you've gotten yourself into."

"You think you see right through me, don't you?"

"That doesn't make me a mind reader, Marcie. We can make love or we can eat dinner or we can unpack. Or we can do all three."

She couldn't stop the grin catching at the corners of her mouth. "At the same time?"

"Now there's a trick. Come on over here and sit down." He patted the bed.

Big hands. A big man. Her eyes wavered between the steady look on his face and the opening in his shirt. "Think we could put some sheets on there? Even roughing it requires some standards."

"Whatever my lady requires. They're in the car. Nice and toasty warm."

But he didn't just walk out and get them. First he placed her hands on his waist. Then he held her face in his hands.

His kiss was gentle but deep. He took his time. Afterwards, he caught his breath. "Be back in a minute."

Her lips were still tingling when he got back. She hadn't moved.

He snapped one of the sheets out over the mattress. She broke into motion as if released from a trance. Bed making was such a mundane task. So homey. "This mattress will cool down these sheets right away."

"Not with us on them."

She ignored it.

"You don't have stretch marks, do you?"

Her mouth gaped open.

"How could I? You know I don't have children."
She stopped, realizing she'd been tricked into
taking him too seriously again. "My body is fine,"
she said stiffly.

"How about letting me be the judge of that."

"I've caught on."

"To what?"

"To you purposely pushing me like this, getting
me to react."

"Getting you hot and bothered?"

She yanked out a corner he'd done and refolded
it properly. "There. You could bounce a quarter
on that."

"How about two good-sized adults?" He tugged
his shirt out of his belt and unbuttoned the rest.
The tail ends lay on his thighs as he sat on the
edge. For him, the stairs weren't necessary. "Are
you going to take your clothes off, or are we going
to have deliberations for another few hours?"

She crossed her arms tighter, clamping them
over her chest. "I'm just not sure we're approaching this the best . . . way."

"Want me to draw you a map?"

"Don't get huffy with me."

"You're stretching my patience. And another
part of my anatomy."

"You're being crude again."

"On purpose."

"To rile me."

"Bet that pretty little behind I am."

Bright circles of pink stood out on her cheeks.

"Marcie, I don't propose to chase you around
the bed, the cabin, or the woods."

"Good."

"All I ask is that you come over here."

"And?"

He sighed, his gaze never leaving hers. "Stop talking and walk."

She took a step. Another. "I'm sorry I'm nervous. I, you—"

"Shhh." He held out his palm. "Give me your hand, that's all you have to do."

She did, feeling foolish, feeling scared. He didn't know how much she was putting on the line, how much this meant to her and how badly she wanted it to be right. And yet, she'd already made a mess of it.

He let her hand rest in his, a rough callus on his thumb caressing her palm. He leaned over and planted a kiss there. She shuddered to her knees. Her ankles felt like wax, their support not at all trustworthy.

He tugged and her hand followed, limp as the arm attached to it. He kissed her wrist, her pulse. Her hand flattened as he laved her skin. He took advantage, pressing it to his cheek, his neck, then the warm mat of hair where his shirt lay open. His voice was as rough as that hair, as tantalizing. "Touch me, Marcie. You lead. We'll do whatever you want, just don't stop touching me."

How could she? He was on fire, and she was drawn to his heat. One hand outside his shirt, one inside, she undid the buttons of his shirt. She counted the hairs on his chest, fingertip by fingertip, then raked the hard nipples with her short nails. She reached inside his collar, turned it down to catch the musky aroma of his aftershave, and slid her palms down his sides. The barrier of a belt sent her hands back up. She stripped his shirt down, baring his arms.

He stood unsteadily, not wanting to frighten her. "Don't stop."

"I haven't."

"It's just I had to—"

"I needed you to." She undid his belt. Put her hands inside and slid them down his narrow hips, feeling the crinkle of hair on his thighs, the muscles larger this time, harder. His briefs came off with the jeans.

He stepped on the back of one short boot, tugging it off, then on the other, kicking the jeans aside. He wanted to get his socks off, but the way she looked at him had him ramrod straight, unable to so much as bend.

"May I?" He was surprised his voice came out at all, although the sound was ragged and forced.

The hint of uncertainty in her eyes showed she wasn't sure what he was asking. She took the chance and nodded anyway.

He lifted her sweater to her armpits, tilted his chin up, a signal to lift her arms over her head.

"How can I if I'm supposed to touch you at all times?"

"Lean forward."

She did, so her cotton shirt was against his bare skin, her denim-clad thighs against his bare legs.

"Feel that?"

She nodded.

"You're touching me."

"So I am," she murmured.

The sweater came off, a shower of golden hair falling once more around her shoulders. She gave her head a shake.

Ray felt it everywhere. He messed up the buttons on her blouse. She took over, finding a way to touch his chest with the backs of her hands as she did so.

"Are you still blond"—he had to swallow to complete the sentence—"everywhere?"

Her smile was her answer. "Your hair was blonder once."

"It's darkened."

"Everywhere?" A coquettish gleam in her eye, she leaned back without stepping away, her thighs balancing against his so the touch would be maintained. She looked down.

"You were practically strawberry blond." A tight accommodating hair curled around her finger. "And you had such a tan from working on those rooftops. Caramel everywhere but this strip where your jeans were." She followed the faint stripe, stopping where her hands met in the back. "It's unbuttoned now."

Ray dragged his attention back to her clothes, the blouse came off her shoulders and dropped. "How am I going to peel you out of those jeans?"

She laughed low. "You like them?"

"They're so tight the brand name's going to be impressed on your behind."

She slunk against him like a cat.

He groaned, exhaling into her hair. "Are you ready for me, Marcie?"

He quaked when her arms went around his neck, when her lips touched his ear. If she answered, he didn't hear it, there was too much thunder. He moved against her, pressing himself into the space low on her abdomen. Her legs parted, one on either side of his thigh.

She hadn't answered, but he wasn't asking much, only everything. To share what they'd had, what they'd always have.

He murmured a name. So did she. The word

love was used, invoked, repeated. *My love. Make love. Please, love.*

The bed was behind him, all he had to do was lower her. In a tangle of arms and legs, they managed. His mouth left hers, tongues untwined only for the time it took to release a harsh breath, a groan, a hiss at her brazen touch. The room was on fire but no one called out. She was his again. His. And he was going to give and give, taking until she was too weak to leave, too convinced of his love to ever doubt. They belonged together, the way he belonged in her.

"Marcie, touch me."

She did.

He breathed a long, shuddering moan then shook his head like a dog out of water, vainly attempting to clear the roar in his ears. "I should never have taught you that."

She chuckled. "I'm a good pupil?"

He buried his face in her strewn hair. "You've got a great memory."

"Plus a little creativity."

He grunted and before he realized it, she had him flat on his back, ministering to his body like a golden angel with a flair for sensuality and no pity whatsoever. "Do you like that?" she teased, but with an edge in her voice, an eagerness.

His face was contorted with the effort of self-control. "Marcie, you're going to make me—"

"You had it planned the other way around. You were going to make me."

"Then stop—oh my—"

He let go of the crushed handful of sheet and dragged her over him, under him. Her heart thundered at the dark, mutinous look in his eyes.

"Not this time," he replied, his voice like gravel.

"This time it isn't for me or you. We're in this together." He lurched off the bed to the dresser. When he came back, she'd pulled the covers up in some incredible notion of modesty.

He looked down on her for a long moment. In full light, the curtains open, the room unshadowed, he stood before her. With one motion, he tore her carefully tucked sheets to the end of the bed, the blankets, all of it until the mattress was bare again. An unset stage was all they needed.

He lowered himself on her, pinning her wrists over her head, watching the way her breasts rose as she arched toward him. "You think I'm going to let you do all the torturing?"

"Exactly what do you have in mind?"

"What I've had in mind since you kicked me out of your life."

"Revenge?" Her mouth was dry, her heart fluttered at the dark intensity in his eyes.

"Do you think I'm capable of that kind of vengeance?"

"I don't know," she answered honestly, her pulse tripping.

He eased into her. Despite the tension in her arms, her legs parted easily. The tightness was elsewhere. He pressed. *I'm here to love you*, he wanted to say. But he had to prove it first, let her trust build even as their passion unraveled all the other inhibitions. "What I want," he said slowly, "is the way your skin squeaks when I rub against you. Like this."

He moved.

She nodded.

He pressed further. An inch, another. Her eyes closed and her mouth opened, a moan escaping through parted lips.

"What I want," Ray whispered, "is a humid night in August. You and me, damp, wasted, unable to move."

He moved.

She tossed her head weakly back and forth on the bare mattress.

He pressed further. All the way.

She arched against him with a cry. She moved.

He didn't. "Tell me you think this is about revenge now."

"No."

"Then say yes. Come with me, Marcie."

"Yes, yes."

They moved together.

It hit him like a battering ram, the soft pant of her voice, the unutterable sensuality. She had his heart beating like a tom-tom. The touch of that stunning, unafraid, explorative girl who'd made him feel like king of the hill, was a woman's now.

They were joined by the slippery friction that started molten, liquid fires. The last of the quilt was kicked to the floor with a *whump* of air, like the breath rushing from his lungs. The wind outside picked up, the chink beneath the window whistled like a teakettle, a boiler about to blow.

He heard her call his name. Asleep, awake, alone, he'd heard that voice in his dreams. He moved, she met, they melted and sizzled and she called his name again as the explosion undid them.

Eleven

Marcie swallowed, her body still humming with his touch, flushed from their passion, and yet her heart felt like a void waiting for his words.

He measured them out carefully. "I've never been one to beg," he said softly. *I was too damn close to begging. So I walked away instead.* "I couldn't be what you wanted then."

"But I did want you, too much."

"Think it would've worked?"

"Probably not."

He looked up at her with a wry grin. "So why have we been tying ourselves in knots over something that happened ten years ago?"

"Because it never really died. There's still something between us."

He touched her cheek. "More than ever, if you ask me."

"I wasn't asking," she said. "I'm telling." Her lips were warm, exploratory.

"What're we going to do about this?"

"Guess."

The fire crackled and spit, the chimney moaned. The rug was scratchy against her back. Tongues and teeth and breath countered, tangy with the thick taste of the dark red wine he'd brought along, the glasses sitting next to them on the floor.

She wanted to reach down, move them out of harm's way. He'd brought such beautiful crystal for a weekend in the wild. How could she not love the man? She took his face in her hands and gave him a shake. "How could you ever think you weren't good enough for me."

"I thought it, believed it, ate it, and breathed it for a year after. Who was I kidding? You were, are, the most beautiful, sexy, rich—"

"Not anymore."

"Leggy, exciting, infuriating, unflappable woman."

"Seriously."

He ran his mouth over her bared breast. "I'd say what we're doing is pretty serious."

Her breath caught as ripples of sensation radiated outward. "Do you—" But her nerve failed her. With all her dignity, training, and inbred tact, she still couldn't come right out and ask a man she'd be sleeping with all weekend if he might love her. "Did you, ever—"

Ray paused. It didn't take a genius to know what she was asking. It only took a dunce this long to figure it out. He bit back a curse at his own insensitivity. "Marcie, I loved you then. I'm sorry you ever doubted it."

"Thank you."

"I love you now."

Her throat was so tight, she had to say thank you with her kiss.

Ray reached for another sip of wine. When he put the glass to her lips, it was warm from the fire.

"We don't need heat," she whispered. "We need contact."

She demonstrated. When her fingertips touched his nipples, he could have sworn they were wired directly to his heart. It beat like a wrecking ball smacking into a tottering brick wall. She got on her knees, her back straight and bare, her spine a subtle ridge his fingers traced until her mouth came in contact with one light brown nub.

For Ray it was pure sensation, a rocket going off in his bloodstream. For Marcie it was a dozen things. Rain ticking on the roof. The sofa beside them smelling of damp and musty horsehair. The rug silted with years of sand, sticking to her in places, abrading. His hands. His heartbeat. His labored breathing.

Eyes half closed, sensations rifling through her, her voice seemed to come from somewhere else. "You make me dance like that inside," she murmured, watching the blurry flames. "The very same way."

He touched her with his tongue, proving her right. When the thundering shocks eventually subsided, she had to close her mouth, wet dry lips, inhale the smells all over again to get her breath. Tart, tangy man and woman smells filled her flaring nostrils.

Later, he fingered her hair. "Whoever spun straw into gold must have gotten the idea from you."

"What does that mean," she asked lazily, a satisfied smile on her lips.

"I don't know. It sounded good."

She chuckled, feeling his body next to hers. "Why do you look so smug?"

"I'm happy. I got everything I ever wanted right here."

Was that all he wanted? There was a twinge near her heart. She ignored it. "I've been thinking."

"You could think through all that? Woman, you're something else."

She swatted at him for making jokes. "Thinking about the future," she said.

The words hung there, like the fog that sat on the icy lake.

"Ours?"

She nodded, glad for once of the darkness, the fire's minimal red glow. If she was taking this too far, expecting too much, better she humiliate herself without him seeing. But the will to remain silent wasn't there. She had to ask, even if it meant rushing in. "What kept us apart before doesn't apply any more. We're both successful. You even more so. If we met now, there'd be nothing to divide us at all."

She listened to him listening, her eyes wide in the dark.

"You're right," he said, his voice low, his emotions difficult to gauge. "If we met now, you'd think I was a completely different man than the one I used to be."

"So there's no problem. No divisions."

"Not class ones. Come to bed. You're going to freeze that cute behind off."

The bed was even colder than the floor. They huddled for warmth. Marcie was wide awake anyway, thinking out loud and setting goals with the man who was going to be there to share them. "We should write this down."

"Did you bring your chalkboard?"

"You're grumpy when you're sleepy, I'll remember that. One: We have to be honest with each other."

"Uh-huh."

"Two: We talk regularly, every night if we have to, about anything that might be bothering us."

"Three," Ray added in a mumble. "We make love regularly, every night if we have to."

"You're making fun of me."

"This isn't the Normandy landing; do we have to plan it all now?"

"Setting goals makes things clearer. It shows you what you want out of life."

"Same old Marcie." He nibbled her shoulder. "What if I know what I want?"

He nipped this time.

"You can't just live for the moment," she said in her best prim tones.

"For these kinds of moments, oh yes I can." Ray slid a hand across her abdomen. "We can work this out tomorrow, when I draw a plat map of your erogenous zones."

They laughed. Soon, Ray slept. Marcie lay awake long into the night, pondering how surrender and triumph could meet in one act, where giving became taking, two bodies one.

She'd sensed his discomfort when it came to talking about the future, and she made a silent vow: He'd never have reason to doubt her or himself. He'd believed he wasn't good enough. A guilty ache told her she'd been part of convincing him of that. No more. She was proud of all she'd accomplished on her own, but not half as proud as she was of Ray.

The line of a song about heroes wafted through

her mind as she drifted to sleep in his arms. She'd tell him he was her hero in the morning.

She slept in. She, who was born with an alarm clock in her head. Sandy always teased her, saying, "Never late, never without a spare sewing kit, an extra tissue, lip balm. Never a hair out of place. . . ." Not today.

Marcie smiled lazily and ran her hands through her hair. It seemed to be everywhere. She ought to hop out of bed in horror and go do something with it before Ray came back. But her arms weren't obeying. They paused over her head, fingers toying with velvety strands.

He'd gotten up at least an hour ago, she'd felt him go. The coolness left behind wasn't as nice as his body, but it was pleasant. She'd had plenty of his body last night. Just the thought—

Pots and pans clanked in the kitchen. She sniffed, then inhaled long and deep, feeling the stretch in her back, her lungs, her ribs, and her breasts. Everything ached slightly. "Because everything," she enunciated lusciously, "got a workout last night."

"You awake?" he called from the other room.

She smiled. Lord, what had come over her? She wasn't even embarrassed to be caught talking to herself. "Lying here naked and sinfully satisfied in a bed two hundred miles from home. Tsk, tsk, Miss Courville."

She heard him humming in the kitchen, aware she hadn't really answered him. Let him think she was asleep a little longer. In fact, she just might drift off for another few minutes. Sandy, after all, raved about David's cooking her breakfast in bed. "Married life . . ." she'd muse, with that smile Marcie envied so much.

Married. She thought it over in the shower. Could they work it out? Perhaps if she remembered her decision to let him know how proud of him she actually was.

A strategy her mother would have approved of. "Show an interest in a man's work," she'd said. "They love that."

Marcie chuckled. To think she was manhunting!

"You in here?" His gruff, low voice gave her a start.

"Yes," she answered quickly, the misty shower door between them.

"Brought you a towel."

"Thanks."

It was fluffy and fragrant, he'd warmed it by the woodstove. The door closed, and he was gone.

"I love him, Mother," Marcie said softly, burying her face in the softness her hard man rarely showed.

Marcie trotted out into the main cabin, aware she was wearing nothing more than one of his shirts, her own lace undies, and some warm socks. Before she could throw her arms around him, she was stopped in her tracks by the sight of the table. "How many pancakes are you making?!"

"Better get something on before Dad comes in."

"Dad?"

"He's here to help open up the cottage."

"Oh." Three place settings accompanied the platters of food. Through the window, she glimpsed another car parked beside theirs.

Theirs. "Does he know?" she asked.

Ray chuckled at the stricken look on her face. "He will soon enough."

The screen squeaked open. Before the kitchen door could follow, Marcie was scrambling into the bedroom to put on something decent. She overheard blunt masculine voices.

"Hey."

"Got the stuff out of the car?"

"Mostly."

"I could give you a hand after breakfast."

"No, son, I'm fine. Your uncle Ted's boys might be up later. But you know them. Might show, might not."

Ray glanced up from the frying pan as Marcie entered a second time. "Dad? I'd like you to meet Marcie."

Marcie plastered on a smile and stepped into the room, hand extended. "Mr. Crane, it's so nice to meet you."

"Uh, hi. Miss." He shook her hand, holding it as if it were fine china.

Marcie beamed. He was almost as tall as Ray, the resemblance strong. They had the same angular, lined face, although the elder Crane was stockier, thicker, less lanky than his son. Ray ducked his head under the hanging kitchen lamp as he spooned out some hash browns.

"Ray mentioned you usually open the cottage on Easter weekend. Will Mrs. Crane be here too?"

His Dad was trying to catch his eye. Ray returned to his fry pan. "She's home with Mitzi. Been taking her back and forth to the doctor all week."

"Oh, I'm so sorry to hear that."

"Mitzi's the dog," Ray put in.

"Loves that damn dog," Mr. Crane added. "Poodle." He practically spit the word. "Suppose if she had grandchildren, she'd chase after them the same way."

Marcie chuckled, genuinely delighted. His Dad was practically blushing. With the spatula, Ray motioned them both to sit.

"Anything I can do?" Marcie offered.

"Just keep charming my Dad," Ray murmured, planting a kiss behind her ear. He shooed her back to the table.

In a few short minutes, she'd smoothly elicited a dozen facts about his family. Ray marveled. Even in a sweatshirt, she looked effortlessly pulled together. The collar of a white cotton blouse was tipped up just so, emphasizing her long neck. Her golden hair was pulled back in a springy ponytail. Sharp, classy. And her behind looked great in those jeans.

He tried to remember how old his own getup was. The jeans dated back at least four years, the chamois shirt was older. It was sturdy and warm, but not exactly L. L. Bean.

She didn't seem to mind. But then, Marcie would be at home in any social setting, including with his family. Unlike him meeting hers, if that had been possible. He disregarded the hint of insecurity as he flipped sausages in a pan.

Anyone who knew Marcie would be shocked, that much was clear. With him, the woman was gayer, friskier, sexier than the careful image she presented to the world. He pictured her prancing into the kitchen just moments ago and wondered why that gave him such a strange feeling of pride.

"You must be very proud of Ray," she said, snapping his attention back to the conversation.

"Oh yeah. He's gone quite a ways since he quit

his uncle Ted's. Course, that was only a summer thing." His Dad happily bragged about Ray's board memberships, the testimonial dinners, the influence he wielded. "Course, he wants to move on over to Derby. Couldn't figure that out, till now." Mr. Crane smiled at Marcie.

Ray swallowed a shot of orange juice. "Dad . . ."

"Hell, he's got me over for lunch at that country club twice a week. And he flies me around in that plane, heh, heh."

"Plane?" Marcie asked, clearly impressed.

Ray grunted and poured more batter into the sizzling pan. He was getting this uncomfortable itch, something nagging at the base of his skull he didn't want to think about.

"He's never let on he was that successful," she murmured. She saw him in a whole new light, that much was clear.

"Not the shingle jockey I used to be," he remarked shortly.

"You've come so far."

"Only to be back where I started." His gaze rested on her, stormy and dark.

Marcie sensed something wrong, but her compliment seemed so harmless. She'd only been trying to say—

His father was speaking again. "You know, I've been kinda wondering about this son of mine. With all he's got, you'd think the girls would be runnin' after him."

"I'm glad they're not," Marcie replied politely, shaken. It wasn't the mention of other women that put this sudden tension in the room. Ray was concentrating on his cooking.

"And what do you do, Marcia?" his father asked.

"It's Marcie," she gently corrected. "Marcie Courville." She reached around the pancakes to shake hands again.

"Courville. Is that so?"

Ray dragged out his chair and sat as if a land mine had been planted on it. "Dig in, folks."

His father cleared his throat, tapped a knife against the corner of his plate, did everything but call his name to get his attention. Ray passed the butter but didn't look up.

"Courville," Mr. Crane repeated softly, more to the air than to either of them, as he got up to tear off a corner of paper towel. "Been sitting here all this time with motor grease on my hand. Can't be making much of an impression, eh son?"

"Don't worry about it."

"You know how it is. Want to look good for the ladies."

Ray glared at his plate, teeth grinding as he chewed. "I know how it is."

When the meal was finished, Ray's father excused himself. "Gotta look at what winter's done to that boat motor. Been sitting out since January."

"Won't hurt it."

"Gotta look all the same." The screen door banged shut behind him.

Marcie had never seen Ray so withdrawn. She sensed this wasn't the time to call him on it. Had she said something wrong? Or was it simply grumpiness? Just because her heart was on the line was no reason to get overly sensitive. "How about if I do the dishes," she offered. "That way you two can look at the motor together."

"All right," Ray said with a grunt. He scraped off the leftovers, stacked plates, and stopped behind her before he left, winding his arms around her waist. "Your hair smells great. I wanted to tell you."

The lighthearted compliment didn't quite dispel his inexplicable mood, but it was a start.

"Thanks. If you weren't such an early bird, you could have helped me wash it in the shower."

"Mmm. Sorry about the company. I thought maybe he'd skip this weekend."

"Nonsense. Your Dad's a sweetheart. Besides, there's a couple things I've been wanting to tell you."

"Like what?" His tongue was toying with the back of her ear.

He smelled like coffee, syrup, sausage—good enough to eat. Despite the previous night, Marcie's appetite was far from sated. "It can wait until we have more time." She gave him a smacking kiss, which quickly became a long, slow exploration.

"Tell me tonight," he drawled, his tone suggesting a hundred scintillating possibilities.

The sound of the door shutting as he left didn't break the spell. Marcie felt his arms around her as she inhaled. When her pony tail brushed the back of her neck, she felt him there too.

"A plane. Board of directors. How many full-time employees?" She knew Crane Corporation was large, but she'd never guessed the extent of it. "Shame on you for not telling me, Raymond." The man needed bragging lessons. And sometime between the kisses and the touches and the eddying breaths, she'd tell him.

*   *   *

"All right, Dad."

"All right what?"

"Can we get this over with?"

"Since when are you so touchy?"

"Since you started pounding the table to get my attention about an hour ago."

"I never."

"Out with it."

His father took a hammer to a stubborn, grime-encrusted shaft. "Think that'll do her?"

"Won't know until we put it in the water."

They worked together loosening parts, cleaning them in solvent, layering clean grease across the mechanism. In time, his father got back to the subject that had been hovering over their work like the wind in the pines overhead.

"So this is the Courville girl."

"Yeah, Dad."

"Same one?"

Ray nodded, a frown creasing his cheeks. "How'd you know?"

"I asked your uncle Ted to keep an eye on you that summer you worked for him."

"Dad, I was twenty-four."

"And coming off that crazy marriage. Then when you came back, you moped around so."

Ray chafed at the word. "I didn't mope."

"I know it," his father said quietly. "I've never seen you that broke up about anything before or since. I just don't—"

"Don't what?" The hammer clanged against the casing. Ray eased up on his grip and his emotions.

"Don't want you getting into something that's burned you before, that's all."

"It's different this time."

"Yeah, I'd say it is."

"What's that supposed to mean?"

"You're kind of on her level now."

"Uh-huh." It was meant to be final, a short grunt of assent to close off the subject. His father had one more thing to add, and although Ray saw it coming, he couldn't avoid it. It was what he'd been thinking, in one way or another, ever since he'd won Marcie back.

"Amazing what a few million will do to raise a woman's opinion of a man."

"She's not a gold digger, Dad."

"Doesn't have to be. You're the one who's climbed on up. You're finally good enough for her."

Twelve

Finally good enough. The words ate at Ray as if he'd swallowed slow-acting acid. His stomach churned.

"Time for bed, sleepyhead." Marcie planted a soft kiss on his temple, a waft of perfume trailing over the back of the sofa as she leaned over it. "Your Dad's been out for an hour."

Ray cracked a smile, listening to the snoring from the loft bedroom. "He turns in early. That's what you get after a lifetime on the morning shift."

"Ah. And are you a night owl?"

A picture of him standing in the dark watching her bedroom window flashed into his mind. In a way he was still looking up. Why couldn't he put that behind him? "Why don't we wait until the fire dies down?"

Marcie curled up at the other end of the sofa, her feet poking under his leg. "In the meantime, mind if I warm up?"

Ray felt a shot of tension, an internal buzz. He

knew that saucy smile. For most of the day he'd been just busy enough tackling odd jobs around the cabin to avoid the inevitable. It was almost eleven. Marcie wasn't going to let him withdraw much longer. Neither was his conscience. They had something they needed to face.

Ray stared at the crackling flames. The blasted bonfire he'd started wouldn't burn down for at least another hour. "I think we should talk," he said to the flames.

Marcie's silence egged him into glancing at her. She didn't look stunned, hurt, or even particularly cautious. She lifted her chin slightly, and her brows. "Yes?"

Ray swung his legs off the sofa and planted his elbows on his knees, the better to pretend he was watching the fire. "About whatever future this thing has. If you're interested."

This thing? Marcie gulped but she managed to do it silently. He was casting around for the right words; what those words would be, she had no idea. Put on a good face, she thought. Be positive. No need to panic yet. Her heart, beating a rapid tattoo, didn't quite get the message. "I think we have a very promising future." It sounded like a year-end report. She pressed her lips firmly together.

Ray said nothing.

She didn't like it, him staring into the flickering light and her out in Siberia, two feet away on the sofa. She scooted up beside him, folding her legs under her. Thigh to thigh, her hand running down his back, she took what strength she could from the muscles there, the warmth, strenuously ignoring the tension.

"Ever worry we don't have enough in common?"

"No. We're very similar at heart."

He scoffed. "I don't see it."

That's because he was looking at the wrong things, the fire, the past. Marcie had to make him see. "We're doers. We set goals and go after what we want. I admired that in you before, the night classes, how hard you worked."

"You never told me you wanted a woodworking shop."

"I didn't know I did. I only knew I had certain things I wanted to accomplish."

"Such as?"

"There was my place as a Courville, that had certain responsibilities. But I also wanted to achieve something. The problem was doing it without turning my back on my family, on who I was."

"I've run into that too. At family picnics people tell me I'm going to be too important to associate with the Cranes much longer. The big shot."

"They're only teasing."

"Yeah, but the message gets across all the same."

"You wouldn't turn your back on people who care about you. I know you." She ran her fingers down his neck in a gentle massage, the ends of her nails scraping softly.

He shuddered, wanted to nod, to keep his mind on talking. He brought her hand around and held it in his. Her nails were perfect, softly rounded, buffed and glossy. Her skin was flawless against his hands, which were cracked in places, roughened by a life of work. No matter how high up he got, he'd never been able to resist picking up a hammer on a job site. "So we're both loyal to our backgrounds, our families."

"That's what I meant about having things in common."

On the contrary, he saw it as compounding their differences. "Was that why you got married, Marcie? Did your family pressure you?"

Marcie rested her chin on his shoulder with a small sigh, hoping this was what was standing between them. If only she could dispel it. "No pressure, they weren't like that. I wanted to please them, thinking it was what I wanted too. Part of my life plan."

Ray hadn't heard that expression in ten years. He'd had a life plan too; he'd asked her to be a part of it. They'd been kids with wild dreams. She was his dream come true. Maybe it was high time he woke up.

The fire spit and sputtered.

"I convinced myself I loved Brad," Marcie said, her carefully modulated voice reverberating in his ear. "We were perfect for each other; he never challenged my goals." She laughed softly. "It took me a long time to realize I need challenges, otherwise I play it too safe. I was doing just that until you came along."

He turned, his profile to her. "So I'm a challenge, am I?"

He was, to every part of her, from her self-image to the reactions he elicited from every inch of her body. "You make me feel things it's safer not to feel. You shake up my foundations."

The breathy voice against his ear made him smile. The sultry words made him ache.

"You make me lose control. This ice princess melts around you, and don't tell me you haven't noticed." She ran a hand down his biceps, squeezing, admiring.

A deep heat was simmering inside him. The woman knew exactly what she was doing. She was wooing him, effortlessly, with élan, with tact. She adjusted as he leaned back against the sofa, balancing her chin on her open palm, her elbow on the sofa back. Looking like a million bucks. Any man would want her. What made him so special?

"Does it all add up now, Marcie? Am I challenging enough? Rich enough? Good enough in bed?"

If he'd slapped her, he couldn't have produced that stunned look. He wanted to take it back, but words didn't work that way.

She moved far enough away to cross her arms over her chest without brushing his shoulder. "You're letting the past intrude again."

"I have to, it's still there. The money's the only thing that's changed us."

No, she wanted to shout at him, scream at him. That was a sign she had to get her emotions under control or they'd have an ugly scene. Very well, if she had to lay her feelings on the line, she would. She could. She'd learned that much this time around. The only difference being the limb she was going out on was higher, flimsier, the drop farther. "I'm very proud of what you've done. You've come a long way."

"And what does that do for us? Where are we in this?"

Together, her heart whispered.

"I see us," she began slowly, "living in Derby. You'll set up Crane Corporation headquarters there, I'll run Designs on the Past."

"We'll join the country club. At least, I'll have to."

"You already belong—"

"—to two others, yeah. Now I'll be a member of Derby's."

"We can live in my condo." She noticed more tension in his jaw, the way he clenched his fist. Signs, signals, why couldn't they say what they felt? Maybe there were no words for it. "We could even look into building something else, if you'd prefer."

"Courville House is your home."

"I had it on the market once."

"Marcie."

"All right, I would like to stay if I could. I love it." *But I love you more.* The words clogged her throat. She had to find something else they could share. "Do you like children?"

"Yes."

"Me too. I'm the end of the line for the Courvilles, but you have more than enough relatives to make up for that." She laughed, hoping he'd join her.

He did, a short rueful laugh. "I'm rich in that, at least."

"You're rich in a lot of things," she murmured.

"I am now."

The words crackled like the logs.

"You always were."

He said nothing. Her heartbeat roared in her ears.

"I left you before. Don't you worry it'll happen again?"

"That was partly my fault."

"You told me to go, I went."

"I only ended up hurting myself, wondering how you could have loved me and just gone."

"I wondered what kind of man would go without a fight. The kind of man I was, I guess."

"Ray, tell me what's wrong."

"Maybe I'm still that man. Unable to measure up no matter how I reach."

"That isn't true!"

His look was like a touch, from her hair to her cheek to her lips. A farewell. "At least we had this much."

Marcie wanted to gulp in the air, run, fight. He was so damned cool about it, withdrawing by the moment and, no matter how she tried, slipping further away. "What am I supposed to do to convince you? Throw things? Break down?" She knew her voice was rising, but she had to reach him somehow. "You weren't wrong for me, I was simply afraid of what you made me feel. I was so different around you, not who I was supposed to be at all. I loved you so much."

He heard the catch in her voice, saw the glint of tears. "It's me I can't convince. Not now, not then. You were beautiful, rich, classy. Who did I think I was kidding?"

"With everything you've done, don't tell me you're insecure."

"You wouldn't know what insecure was," he replied softly, rising from the sofa.

Insecure? She felt it every time she didn't know what he was thinking, every time he turned his back on her.

He studied the flames. "Maybe every man has a weakness, something he's unsure of. With me it's you." He cleared his throat gruffly, his eyes narrowing. "My money, my contacts were supposed to make all the difference."

The man he'd been hadn't had the guts to fight for her, to drag her off the pedestal he'd put her on.

The man he was now was too aware of the

costs. He'd lived a lifetime wanting what he couldn't have. Why gamble and lose? Wasn't it better to walk away from the table now? he asked himself.

"Ray, please talk to me."

"What'll it change?" He grimaced. He knew he was hurting her, not as much as he would if they let it drag on. It was better to end it now, live in reality, not dreams. "Would another million make the difference? Two? Tell me how much it takes before I'm up there with you."

"No!" She covered her ears with her hands. Dragging them down immediately, she crossed her arms over her chest. She had to get herself under control, or she'd be sobbing at his feet. "You're so wrong. We may not have background in common, but we have drive, personality."

"Love." His soft word hit her like a fist.

She collected herself as best she could, feeling pieces breaking off, scattering around the room. She paced to the edge of the rag rug, fighting the irrational feeling that with every step the abyss between them was growing larger until there was no jumping it, no shouting across the silence.

Ray was staring at the fire, telling himself she'd be okay. Marcie could handle things like this. Not like him. His insides felt as if he'd swallowed a bucket of buckshot.

"Do you want me to go?" she asked.

He didn't, but saying it would mean looking at her. Saying it would mean taking her, loving her, following her into the bedroom where she was pulling out her suitcase, throwing clothes in it in crumpled handfulls. Stopping her now would mean seizing what little they had for as long as he could, blinding himself to their differences.

Any other woman could love him for his money, some had. Not Marcie. He wanted her to love him for what he was, not what he'd done. He couldn't risk it any other way. What it came down to was pride, and he knew it.

The moon was bright, the air humid and warm. A layer of fog drifted over the ice and into the trees. Marcie was afraid, but not of the dark. What she feared was the quaver in her voice. "Ray?"

He followed her out the cabin door. She almost hoped he'd take the suitcase out of her hand. He let her toss it in the back seat.

"What can I do? Tell me what to say, I'll say it." Marcie felt a physical pain. "What am I supposed to change?"

"Not a thing." He touched her hair, almost against his will as if, once touched, it would be impossible to bring his hand back. With effort, he managed. "I guess we were wrong to try again."

The wind whispered around them, a pining, yearning sound of words unsaid. Marcie looked into Ray's eyes, so afraid he saw only her perfect surface—blond, blue eyed, unreal, unfeeling. "If I yelled? Argued? Begged?" The last word was a shred of sound, a branch snapping.

"Don't. Consider it my fault. Hate me if you have to." He knew the gamut of emotions all too well when love fell apart. Whatever got you through the night. There'd be a lot of nights to come. He turned toward the porch.

"Wait." She couldn't hold up her hand to stop him, it would have shaken too hard. She looked

at him as long as she dared. She'd been living on
memories for so long, what were a few more?

He gave her an empty look she felt to her soul.
Why? Why had she been foolish enough to fall
in love with the one man she couldn't have? A
man who demanded everything, but didn't have
the confidence to give in return?

She closed her eyes against the pain and took
a staggering step toward the car. "How will I get
back?"

"Take the Mercedes," he said.

She heard the soft crackle of pine needles under
his feet as he stepped toward her. She could
barely make out his hand in the dark, the glitter
of the key. So that was that. "How will you—?"

"Dad will take me. Just leave it outside your
shop, I'll pick it up."

He'd have to come by. She'd see him again. A
thread, a glimmer of hope. To think she'd been
reduced to snatching at such straws. It was as
bad as leaving something behind on purpose so
she could come back for it. Like her heart.

The rev of the engine was like a blade cutting
through him. Ray watched her go, a punishment
he deserved.

Satisfied? An ugly, smirking voice came from
some dark corner of his brain. This time he'd
sent *her* packing.

A nearby tree trunk looked all too inviting to
his fist. Sheer willpower kept his hands in his
pockets. He listened for the fading sound of the
car.

It would have ended sooner or later. He should
be proud of forcing the issue, facing up to it. So

why was he kicking himself? Every word he'd said was true. The past couldn't be undone, there was no way to go back and make her see him for himself alone, to detach that from what he'd done. The ironic part was, he'd done it for her, so he could come back some day and win her. His pride wouldn't let him keep her.

"Idiot!" A blistering series of curses ricocheted in the dark. His teeth ground like the faraway gears of the Mercedes. He hadn't even asked if she knew the way to the main road. Logging roads cut every which way. She could have a flat. When was the last time he'd checked the tires? What about bears? When did they come out of hibernation?

He could have laughed at his wild imagination, if he hadn't been so busy slamming back into the cabin and digging through his dad's jacket pocket for the truck keys.

"Son?"

His father lowered the stair ladder from the loft.

"I'm going into town," Ray said curtly.

"There is no town at this hour. They roll up the sidewalks."

"I meant Derby."

His dad paused halfway down the ladder. When he reached the floor, a quick sweep of the bedroom told him Marcie had cleared out. "Lovers' quarrel?"

"Idiot's delight. With me as the idiot."

"You taking the four-wheel drive?"

"If you don't mind."

"Just leave me enough food to last me. Suppose I could always dig a hole in the ice for fish."

"I won't strand you here. I'll call one of Ted's kids. They might be coming up anyway, right? If

I have to, I'll come back myself. I shouldn't have let her take off alone."

Suddenly, the sound of an engine grew nearer. His heart lurched. She was coming back.

A flood of images goaded him with hope. She'd throw her arms around him, maybe burst into tears. Even if she didn't, he'd apologize. He'd been wrong. He didn't deserve her, that much was clear, but he loved her. If she'd take him back, he'd make it up to her. His only regret was he'd put them both through hell to get to the other side of his pride.

The lights cut through the trees, coming fast. Ray strode out to the end of the drive, determined to make it up to her.

The car screeched to a halt half a foot in front of his knees.

"What're you doing standing in the middle of the drive!" Johnny, one of his uncle Ted's boys asked. The others piled out.

"Hey Ray! How ya doin'?"

"Ray! Didn't know you'd be here."

"If I get a dent in this from running you down, Merilee'll never forgive me. For the dent, I mean."

Johnny gave him a hug. Mike and Ed proceeded to unload sleeping bags. "You probably got the bed staked out. Where's Uncle Bill?"

"Inside." It was the only word Ray said, and as short as his temper. Somewhere a screen door opened and shut.

"Hiya, Uncle Bill."

"Boys."

"Who was that we almost ran into on the road?"

Ray's gut tightened. "Ran into?"

"Thought it was you for a minute. Some guy going the other way in a Mercedes."

"Down our road."

"Musta been lost."

"Drunk probably. Didn't know the road, anyway."

"Weaving?" Ray asked. She was probably crying. Another slam of recriminations ran through him. He should never have let her go alone.

"Why else would anyone be way out here this time of night? Unless he was lookin' for the Lumberjack Bar."

Ray cursed as the screen slapped shut behind him. He was going after her, that's all there was to it. He threw his clothes in his own suitcase and hunched into his leather jacket. "Of all the low-life, two-bit scum. Sending a woman out alone this time of night, driving roads she doesn't know, with drunks from the Lumberjack Bar out on the streets. Hell, it'll be four in the morning before she gets to Derby." If she got there.

Did she have a credit card with her? Would she stop somewhere for the night? Could she even see straight? He damn well couldn't.

When he came back out, his dad and the boys were talking quietly beside Jake's sedan.

"Hey Ray."

"Going after her?"

Ray stopped in his tracks and glared at his father. "Yeah."

"Happy hunting."

His father's old four-wheel—drive truck bounded over the ruts and careened around the trees. He was almost as hard on the shocks as on himself.

"Big man. Going to win her back. Get around her defenses. Never noticed you had defenses too." And he'd stumbled over them like a two-year-old learning to walk.

"You don't deserve her. You never deserved her."

That wasn't going to stop him. Last time, maybe. This time almost. Never again.

If he wanted her to love him, the money and everything else was part of it. That explained a lot as he made it out to the highway and took off south. For ten years he'd been scratching and clawing and climbing out of a pit, reaching for the light, working his way back to Marcie.

He wasn't going to slip back now.

Thirteen

It rained. Crouched on the side of I-75 changing the truck tire, the crowbar slipped, and he scraped his knuckles on the rusted wheel rim. Better it should happen to him than her. It didn't matter that it was two o'clock in the morning and no other motorists were in sight, he'd handle it. There was a churning in his gut; it had been there most of the day, but it was a steady burning by now. In a way it reminded him of those first years at Crane Corporation, when he'd had no other options. He was determined to make it. What he was after was too important.

But Marcie wouldn't see him. Sandy took messages at the shop. Ray wondered if they ever got through. It would've been easy to conjure up meddlesome interference, but he wasn't into dreams anymore. He had to face the possibility that Marcie was coldly looking at every telephone note that Sandy passed on, crumpling them in her carefully manicured fingers.

Didn't matter. She loved him. He intended to remind her of that fact, as soon as he kissed that hurt look off her face and took the pain out of her eyes.

The Mercedes was parked beside the carriage house. He let it sit, part of the plan.

By the end of the week, the town's two cab drivers knew him by name. By the end of two, they knew where he was going without being told. He visited every new subdivision and cul-de-sac, cruised each tree-lined street of old Victorian homes. He wanted a house, he said, but it was hard to explain to a realtor that it had to be the perfect house, some place he could take Marcie and get down on one knee and convince her he wanted to make a family with her, whether it was the two of them or ten kids. He hadn't found the spot yet, but he knew he would. He had to.

The drivers knew this much, every excursion ended with a loop up the hill past Courville House.

"Could you swing around by that little shop in back?"

"Don't I always?" the driver muttered goodnaturedly. "They got some condos up here. Don't know if that's what you're looking for."

Ray was looking for a hint that Marcie was there. The driver's words murmured in the background like engine noise. He'd heard enough real-estate advice to last him a lifetime. He hadn't heard word one from Marcie.

They cleared the crest of the hill. It was mid-April, sunny and sixty degrees. A sign in her shop window said OPEN; the doors were spread wide. He leaned forward in the seat, hoping to catch sight of her. A woman in an apple-green smock walked by the doorway just as they passed. Ebony hair. Alexandra. Ray unclenched the back of the driver's seat.

"That wouldn't be your Mercedes, would it? Heard tell you had a bronze one." The driver managed to look him up and down in the mirror. Ray watched him add together the tailored suit, the leather attaché case, and the watch. They equaled bronze Mercedes.

"Yeah, it's mine."

"Someone steal it?"

"I gave it away."

The man's eyes widened before darting back to the road.

Ray cringed at the sound of his own words. What kind of tip did a man who gave away Mercedes give?

In keeping with that thought, the driver was more than willing to obey any command. "Want to go around again?"

Ray sighed and slumped against the seat. "No thanks." And yet, as they headed down the hill, he looked back, cursing himself all the while. He was acting like a lovesick teenager. Next thing he knew, he'd be standing under her bedroom window at night waiting for a glimpse of her. He had the sensation of having come full circle, right back to where he'd started. And no, he didn't want to go around again.

"Open house," the driver was saying.

"Hmm?"

"Not exactly the split-level executive style you've been looking at, if you don't mind my saying. But you can't beat the location. Location, location, location, that's what you need in real estate."

"So I've heard."

"These are supposed to be some of the ritziest in town."

"Yeah, they are. Stop!"

"What? Here?" He hit the brakes.

Ray suddenly saw it, the sign, the answer. He could break the cycle right now. "I'll get out here."

"It's a couple miles back to town, bud."

"Back up the hill they're selling condos."

"That's what I been saying all this time."

"Just drop me off." He peeled a twenty from his wallet and stopped all argument.

Marcie gulped another cup of Moroccan coffee, wishing her nerve ends were as deadened to it as were her taste buds. A car went by. Her heart beat faster. It was only a taxi.

Sandy hung up the phone. "April showers bring home remodeling, I swear. That builders' show has us lined up for a month in estimates alone."

Marcie swallowed past the lump in her throat. She'd opted out of attending most of the weekend show. What if Ray had attended? She'd hoped he would and prayed he wouldn't. But one look at the scale model exhibit of the new mall had been enough to send her back to the shop for the rest of the day. "I'll hold down the fort there in case we get any calls," she'd said. What a coward. She hadn't answered the phone in two weeks just in case it was Ray.

"Earth to Marcie," Sandy cooed.

"Sorry." She dragged her attention away from the road and back to the office. The taxi had turned into the main drive. Must be an out of towner to see the condos, she thought. They were being snapped up so fast.

"Earth to Mar-cieeee."

"Sorry. Was I doing it again?"

Her partner joined in her laughter. "Better."

"Better than what," Marcie asked, mystified.

"At least you remember how to imitate a human laugh. Last week you couldn't do that."

Marcie grimaced and went back to the estimate she was working on on the minicomputer. Her attention span was pitiful. To listen to Sandy, her complexion was just as bad, as were her energy level, her sleeping habits, and the lifelessness of her hair. She needed a vacation, a massage. She needed a shrink. She needed a man, but only one came to mind.

She closed her eyes against the sudden pain. It hadn't gone away. But it simply had to. She wasn't going to spend the rest of her days aching like this. She was a doer. She set goals. And yet, whatever she decided lately seemed to evaporate before she could so much as write it down.

Like the phone messages. He left his name and number, that was all. Should she call? It was ridiculous to have Sandy answer or to use the machine. She came in early every morning to push the button, hoping to hear his voice, knowing hers would never hold up if she had to talk to him. Oh, you are a coward, Marcie Courville.

What did he want? To apologize? Dream on. He probably wanted his Mercedes delivered. Part of her wished he'd ask for just that. If he proved himself a total cad, she could get angry. She could fill that car with cement from the paving crew who'd finished up the parking area. She could drive it right up his drive and let it harden, along with her heart.

The computer beeped repeatedly. Marcie paid

attention for approximately fifteen seconds. The meticulously constructed facade she presented to the world hadn't clicked back into place the way she'd hoped. There were pieces missing, gaps. Sandy saw through them; how many other people had? This weekend she'd gone to Mrs. Harding's to give an estimate. She'd been asked to sit down, given tea, more or less patted on the hand. What was she, an invalid? Did everyone know she was falling apart?

The computer beeped again. "Shucks!"

"Language, language," Sandy chuckled.

A car came up the hill. Marcie concentrated on the screen before her until the green letters were imprinted on her memory. The car slowed, then continued until it turned into the main drive. Her shoulders sagged.

She had work, responsibilities. Wasn't that what she lived for? To tend to a thousand and one details effortlessly. Poised. In command. Heck, she'd gotten out of her marriage with less hassle. But she'd never missed Brad, never so much.

It was all Ray's fault. He brought out a side of her no one else had. Losing him meant losing the woman who flourished when she was near him. He accepted her completely, even the parts she didn't always accept herself. It was ironic. She'd made such strides in accepting that emotional, irrational part of herself, and yet he was the one who couldn't accept himself!

Marcie looked around the shop as if she'd never seen it before. "That works two ways, you know."

"Okay," Sandy said, brushing back a streak of hair. "What planet are we on now?"

"The man makes me furious!"

"Good. I want to hear you cuss some more."

"I never showed my feelings to anyone the way I did to him."

"So?"

"So I'm not the problem here. He is."

"A loyal friend will always agree with you on that one."

"I'm serious. He's the one refusing to take a chance, refusing to take risks. After all of his pushing me to show my emotions, to open up, he clams up like a, like a—"

"Clam."

"Thank you. And I don't think it's fair."

Sandy shimmied her work stool over to Marcie's computer. "Want to plot out loud?"

Marcie straightened her shoulders a bit. "He's slunk off to lick his wounds. He thinks he's not good enough. Ha! As long as he cares, I can get him back."

"Oh he cares, otherwise he'd claim the Mercedes. Unless he has a spare. Forget I said that."

"I plan to. He's not the only insecure person in the world, or the only determined one." Marcie sealed her vow with a short nod of her head. But her confidence quickly ebbed, seeping out of the room like the afternoon light.

"So what now?" Sandy asked.

Marcie narrowed her eyes, tapping her lower lip with a pencil. "Call Joslyn's. I want an alarm put on that car."

"So that if he sneaks back to pick it up in the middle of the night, you can grab him? Wonderful!"

"Not at all, Alexandra," Marcie said haughtily. "It's simply a valuable automobile, and I don't want to be responsible for it. I have a business to run."

Sandy slapped the phone book on the counter

with a snort. "It's a mantrap, and I say happy hunting."

"I want this unit."

"I'm afraid this one is taken, sir."

"What would it cost to untake it?"

Ray and the realtor spoke in unison. "There *is* another unit available."

"Exactly," Ray countered. "Sell the other one to whoever wanted this one."

The realtor was a little man in a snazzy European suit. He twitched his mustache when his interest was piqued, much like a mouse scenting cheese. Ray hid a grin while he looked up the grand staircase and fought the urge to loosen his tie. He was the big cheese now.

They were one unit over from Marcie's, in what used to be the central hall. It was now the most imposing of the condos at Courville House, as the realtor quickly pointed out.

"However, with three bedrooms, four baths, and a small ballroom on the second floor, it would be rather large for one person."

"Plenty of space for a growing family," Ray replied.

The realtor's eyes lit up. "If your wife is coming through later, I'd be happy to show her the remaining unit as well. Who knows, she may prefer—"

"I don't have a wife, and I intend to buy this unit."

"But you mentioned a family—"

"I intend to have one of those as well." Ray mounted the stairs. MacArthur himself couldn't have strode up a beach with more determination. "A ballroom, huh?"

He was conquering Marcie Courville, not the Philippines, though he couldn't have said which was more difficult. He'd win her back with gentleness and ironclad persistence. He didn't know how many chances a man had in life, but he liked making his own. He had her love, now he needed her forgiveness.

He'd learned a simple, painful lesson: The woman mattered more than his pride. Everything he'd achieved meant nothing without her. What better way to show her he'd conquered his insecurity than by moving into Courville House? His long climb had been to the top of this hill, and he planned on living there even if walls separated them. "Walls can be knocked down," he muttered aloud.

"Any redecorating would be up to you, of course." The realtor waited in the doorway, no doubt convinced by the way Ray commanded the high-ceilinged room that he was a man who got what he wanted.

Ray paced off the dozen mirrors. "We'll dance in here. Just the two of us. I'll put in a CD player, hidden speakers, a rose in a Ming vase. Then I'll invite her over."

What would she do when she discovered who her new neighbor was? Throw the vase at him. Hell, she might bodily eject him from the house. Ray smiled. Grappling with Marcie in a temper wasn't such a bad prospect. Anything was better than her silence. That would end, as soon as his plans were in place.

"If I pay cash, how soon can we close?" Money. He'd worked so hard to earn it, it was about time he put it to good use.

"On this unit?" The realtor loosened his own tie and did some quick math in his head.

"I'll knock that wall out, make a door."

"Uh, that's the connecting wall, sir. Another owner lives there."

"She won't mind."

The realtor's mustache twitched again. It was clear he saw objections, but not enough to spoil a cash sale. "Perhaps you can work that out after closing."

"I'd like to make an offer."

"I'd be more than happy to present it."

A hitch in his plans. Marcie would see his name on any written offer. She'd know. He altered his strategy midgame. "I'd like her response as soon as possible."

"We could make it contingent on a twenty-four hour response."

"She works out back, doesn't she? Get her up here, and we'll settle this right now."

The realtor scurried away, giving Ray a few minutes to compose himself, recompose himself, and look for holes in his plan.

He spent most of those moments walking the length of the ballroom, listening to his footsteps, gazing into the shine on the inlaid wood floor. He stopped in front of one of the mirrors and moved the knot in his tie up a notch. He combed his hair. No sooner was the comb back in his suit pocket than he ruined the effect by running his hands through it.

The suit was his best. To think he'd once had a good suit reserved for meeting with bankers. Now he owned a closet full. But how many times did he get home from work and throw on jeans and an old shirt? Marcie would know that. Just as she'd know that weekends at the cabin were as important to him as dates at the country club. No other woman knew his past, where he'd come from or how far. It wasn't something to be ashamed of, it was something to share, up to and including the foolish pride that had almost torn them apart.

"Excuse me. The realtor tells me you're interested in making an offer."

Ray turned.

Marcie stopped in midstride, her lips parted.

"Marcie Courville, I'll see you in court."

She was stunned to see him, speechless, elated. Marcella Courville, you are not going to burst into tears. Neither are you going to jump for joy, run into his arms, or scratch his eyes out.

She worked her fingers loosely together in front of her when she'd rather be making fists. Even fury could hide behind patrician ways. "May I ask what this is all about?"

He took one hand out of a pocket and hitched a thumb in the direction of the mirrors. "I'm knocking out this wall."

Marcie's eyes couldn't have been wider if he'd had the hammer in his hand. "What exactly are you proposing?"

Proposing, now there was a word. Ray only hoped they'd get to it before she kicked him out. He walked toward her. No matter how his brain told him to take it slow, his body wasn't buying it. He'd been away from her too long, driving himself crazy wanting to see her. He had to play this scene right, and that meant getting to the point.

"I'm buying this unit," he said again, "and I hereby propose, no, I swear, that I'm going to knock down any and every wall that stands between us." He touched her shoulders, her arms. She looked pale. He didn't like those smudges under her eyes. Very carefully, he traced them with his thumbs. From there he framed her delicate face with his hands. "Separate bedrooms is one thing, separate residences is out of the question." He stopped just short of kissing her. "Come to think of it, so are separate bedrooms."

Marcie's heart resounded with a beat never heard in this ballroom. Her lips felt papery and dry, but she couldn't seem to make her tongue wet them. She was only now catching her breath, and his mouth was lowering to hers.

Her lips parted, slightly. His mouth was warm, gentle, questioning. He ended the kiss and waited for her reaction.

He was doing it again, she realized. Pushing buttons, waiting for her emotions to set the tone. Not this time. She'd use these emotions of hers when she was good and ready, even though holding back at this moment felt like the equivalent of reining in a runaway stagecoach. "You can afford it, I take it?"

"I want to spend my money on something besides I beams."

Her eyes flashed. "If you're insinuating that presents and jewels and what-all nonsense is going to win me over—"

He put up both hands in surrender. "I'm the gold digger, not you. I dug it myself, hoping I could impress you with it."

"I was impressed," she said evenly. "With what you've accomplished, not what you have. I tried to tell you."

"I know." His voice cut through the room urgently. "I never lied to you, Marcie, I was lying to myself. I told myself success had nothing to do with you. But those first few years, when every payroll was a crisis, I stayed away. After your divorce I told myself I wouldn't contact you. We were almost bankrupt from overexpansion at the time. I refused to see the connection. Only when the company grew more secure, when I could afford the kind of headquarters I had in mind, that's when I came back.

"The vow says for richer or poorer—who was I to say richer didn't count? Only a fool would be ashamed of success. Like me."

"Then why?"

"I wanted you to love me for who I am. Well, here I am."

She twisted away from him, her eyes rapidly scanning the room, her hands in knots.

"Looking for something to throw?"

"No!" She strode to the French doors. "Actually, I've been thinking these last few days, of letting the clutch out on the Mercedes. It would roll down the hill to the river."

"It'd have to plow through a few trees to get there."

"So much the better."

He winced and grinned. "Come at me with it, Marcie. Let's get all of it into the open."

She shrugged, her hands fluttering at her sides in an over elaborate display of nonchalance. "You think I care?"

"More than you show," he said softly.

She turned on him. "Damn you!" Her cracked voice echoed in the cavernous room. "I showed you more than any other man, and you threw it back in my face!"

"Go ahead, hit me."

She was clearly affronted. "I never stoop to violence!"

"Then you'll just have to forgive me."

She glared at him, her eyes wavering at the daring in his. She knew he was goading her. But how could she resist when all she wanted was to rush into his arms? They'd both made mistakes. There was nothing to forgive. "How can I?"

He cut off her words, not wanting to hear a *no*. Striding to the dusty radio left behind by the construction crew, he switched it on. "Then dance with me."

A sappy love song from the seventies. It'd have to do. He took her in his arms.

He felt so good, so strong. She let her breasts touch his chest. His lips brushed her hair.

"I'm sorry," he whispered.

"Ray."

"Don't. I don't want to argue. I knew when I came here you might not accept it."

"Then why did you come?"

"I had to."

She couldn't look up. His chin pressed the top of her head; her cheek felt entirely too good against his chest. She watched them moving in the mirrors. The top of her head was barely to his shoulder, but the sway of their bodies was perfectly matched.

"What else can I tell you? I was adolescent and insecure, holding onto old hurts. I thought I was over it a long time ago, but when I saw you again and paired myself up with the most beautiful woman in the world . . . insecurity dies hard."

"And your answer is for me to throw something at it."

"At least stomp on it."

She laughed, but from somewhere the tears sprang free. She turned away.

"No," he tipped her chin back to him. "We're being honest this time, don't hide."

She pulled the handkerchief from his breast pocket and wiped her nose. "I may be a little more emotional around you, Lord knows it's probably some hormonal thing, but there are some things I don't advertise." She honked into the handkerchief. "I may be less reserved around you, even less dignified—"

"More sexy, more stimulating, incredibly exciting—"

"Yes, but that's only part of it. I'll never be all that. I'll never be warm or effusive or, or Italian!" She threw up her hands in a melodramatic gesture that had him hiding a grin.

"Uh, I don't think we have to worry about that. But you're making progress."

"And you're the only man I do that with."

"Not to mention a few other things."

"Don't joke. I lose control around you, and you know it."

"All the more reason I should be there to catch you when you fall."

"Fall in love?"

His grin faded. "I'll be there," he said solemnly. "Until time ends or this house falls down around us. Forgive me."

"I do."

The kiss was long and slow, full of promises made and promises kept, debts owed and debts to be repaid on a thousand long nights to come.

The realtor shuffled in and out again. Marcie had to swallow, sigh, and think a moment before she could remember what she wanted to say.

"You mentioned seeing me in court? I take it we've reached a settlement, sir?"

"Uh-uh. I'm taking you in as soon as its legally possible."

"The charge?"

"Driving without a license."

"I have a license."

"Not to drive me crazy. There's only one kind of license for that, and only one man to give it to us. I've been thinking of Judge Rosen."

"From the trial?"

"He got us into this. He's the perfect man to make it permanent."

Marcie had her own opinions on the perfect man, but she wasn't in the mood to argue. "Wedding in here, reception in the garden?"

"Sounds perfect."

She put her head against his shoulder, swaying to another song. The music didn't matter, only that Ray was holding her. "I always dreamed of that."

She pictured the flowers, the folding chairs, the quartet on the raised platform in the corner. Light would stream in over the balcony, the wall of French doors would be thrown open the way Ray liked it.

"Marcie," he said. His voice was husky, an unaccustomed tightness in his throat. "I may never be good enough for you, but I'll never let you regret loving me. I promise."

"Hush." Rising up on tiptoe, she held his face securely in her hands. Then she kissed him fiercely, possessively, merely a hint of what was to come. "I love a man named Ray Crane, and no one is ever going to say a bad word about him in my presence, you included. Got that?"

He nodded, with a little help from her hands.

THE EDITOR'S CORNER

It's a pleasure to return to the Editor's Corner while Susann Brailey is away on maternity leave, the proud mother of her first child—a beautiful, big, healthy daughter. It is truly holiday season here with this wonderful addition to our extended "family," and I'm delighted to share our feelings of blessings with you . . . in the form of wonderful books coming your way next month.

First, let me announce that what so many of you have written to me asking for will be in your stockings in just thirty days! Four classic LOVESWEPT romances from the spellbinding pen of Iris Johansen will go on sale in what we are calling the **JOHANSEN JUBILEE** reissues. These much-requested titles take you back to the very beginning of Iris's fabulous writing career with the first four romances she wrote, and they are **STORMY VOWS, TEMPEST AT SEA, THE RELUCTANT LARK,** and **BRONZED HAWK.** In these very first love stories published in the fall and winter of 1983, Iris began the tradition of continuing characters that has come to be commonplace in romance publishing. She is a true innovator, a great talent, and I'm sure you'll want to buy all these signed editions, if not for yourself, then for someone you care about. Could there be a better Christmas present than an introduction to the love stories of Iris Johansen? And look for great news inside each of the JOHANSEN JUBILEE editions about her captivating work coming in February, **THE WIND DANCER.** Bantam, too, has a glorious surprise that we will announce next month.

Give a big shout "hooray" now because Barbara Bowell is back! And back with a romance you've requested—**THE LAST BRADY,** LOVESWEPT

(continued)

#444. Delightful Colleen Brady gets her own romance with an irresistibly virile heartbreaker, Jack Blackledge. He's hard to handle—to put it mildly—and she's utterly inexperienced, so when he needs her to persuade his mother he's involved with a nice girl for a change, the sparks really fly. As always, Barbara Boswell gives you a sweet, charged, absolutely unforgettable love story.

A hurricane hits in the opening pages of Charlotte Hughes's **LOUISIANA LOVIN'**, LOVESWEPT #445, and its force spins Gator Landry and Michelle Thurston into a breathlessly passionate love story. They'd been apart for years, but how could Michelle forget the wild Cajun boy who'd awakened her with sizzling kisses when she was a teenager? And what was she to do with him now, when they were trapped together on Lizard Bayou during the tempest? Fire and frenzy and storm weld them together, but insecurity and pain threaten to tear them apart. A marvelous LOVESWEPT from a very gifted author!

SWEET MISCHIEF, LOVESWEPT #446, by Doris Parmett is a sheer delight. Full of fun, fast-paced, and taut with sexual tension, **SWEET MISCHIEF** tells the love story of sassy Katie Reynolds and irresistible Bill Logan. Bill is disillusioned about the institution of marriage and comes home to his childhood friend Katie with an outrageous proposition. . . . But Katie has loved him long enough and hard enough to dare anything, break any rules to get him for keeps. Ecstasy and deep emotion throw Bill for a loop . . . and Katie is swinging the lasso. **SWEET MISCHIEF** makes for grand reading, indeed. A real keeper.

Bewitching is the first word that comes to mind to
(continued)

describe Linda Cajio's LOVESWEPT #447, **NIGHTS IN WHITE SATIN.** When Jill Daneforth arrives in England determined to get revenge for the theft of her mother's legacy, she is totally unprepared for Rick Kitteridge, an aristocrat and a devil of temptation. He pursues her with fierce passion—but an underlying fear that she can never be wholly his, never share more than his wild and wonderful embraces. How this tempestuous pair reconciles their differences provides some of the most exciting reading ever!

Witty and wonderful, **SQUEEZE PLAY,** LOVESWEPT #448, from beloved Lori Copeland provides chuckles and warmth galore. As spontaneous as she is beautiful, Carly Winters has to struggle to manage her attraction to Dex Mathews, the brilliant and gorgeous ex-fiance who has returned to town to plague her in every way . . . including competing in the company softball game. They'd broken up before because of her insecurity over their differences in everything except passion. Now he's back kissing her until she melts, vowing he loves her as she is . . . and giving you unbeatable romance reading.

Sweeping you into a whirlwind of sensual romance, **LORD OF LIGHTNING,** LOVESWEPT #449, is from the extraordinary writer, Suzanne Forster. Lise Anderson takes one look at Stephen Gage and knows she has encountered the flesh-and-blood embodiment of her fantasy lover. As attracted to her as she is to him, Stephen somehow knows that Lise yearns to surrender to thrilling seduction, to abandon all restraint. And he knows, too, that he is just the man to make her dreams come true. But her fears collide with his . . . even as they show

(continued)

each other the way to heaven . . . and only a powerful love can overcome the schism between this fiercely independent schoolteacher and mysterious geologist. **LORD OF LIGHTNING**—as thrilling a romance as you'll ever hope to read.

Six great romances next month . . . four great Iris Johansen classics—LOVESWEPT hopes to make your holiday very special and very specially romantic.

With every good wish for a holiday filled with the best things in life—the love of family and friends.

Sincerely,

Carolyn Nichols

Carolyn Nichols,
Publisher,
LOVESWEPT
Bantam Books
666 Fifth Avenue
New York, NY 10103

P.S. GIVE YOURSELF A SPECIAL PRESENT: CALL OUR LOVESWEPT LINE 1-900-896-2505 TO HEAR EXCITING NEWS FROM ONE OF YOUR FAVORITE AUTHORS AND TO ENTER OUR SWEEPSTAKES TO WIN A FABULOUS TRIP FOR TWO TO PARIS!

FOREVER LOVESWEPT

SPECIAL KEEPSAKE EDITION OFFER

$12⁹⁵ VALUE

Here's your chance to receive a special hardcover Loveswept "Keepsake Edition" to keep close to your heart forever. Collect hearts (shown on next page) found in the back of Loveswepts #426-#449 (on sale from September 1990 through December 1990). Once you have collected a total of 15 hearts, fill out the coupon and selection form on the next page (no photocopies or hand drawn facsimiles will be accepted) and mail to: Loveswept Keepsake, P.O. Box 9014, Bohemia, NY 11716.

FOREVER LOVESWEPT
SPECIAL KEEPSAKE EDITION OFFER
SELECTION FORM

Choose from these special Loveswepts by your favorite authors. Please write a 1 next to your first choice, a 2 next to your second choice. Loveswept will honor your preference as inventory allows.

♡ ♡ ♡ *Loveswept* ®

_____ BAD FOR EACH OTHER   Billie Green

_____ NOTORIOUS   Iris Johansen

_____ WILD CHILD   Suzanne Forster

_____ A WHOLE NEW LIGHT   Sandra Brown

_____ HOT TOUCH   Deborah Smith

_____ ONCE UPON A TIME...GOLDEN
       THREADS   Kay Hooper

Attached are 15 hearts and the selection form which indicates my choices for my special hardcover Loveswept "Keepsake Edition." Please mail my book to:

NAME:_____

ADDRESS:_____

CITY/STATE:_____ ZIP:_____

Offer open only to residents of the United States, Puerto Rico and Canada. Void where prohibited, taxed, or restricted. Allow 6 - 8 weeks after receipt of coupons for delivery. Offer expires January 15, 1991. You will receive your first choice as inventory allows; if that book is no longer available, you'll receive your second choice, etc.